NOT ANYWHERE,

JUST NOT

KEN SPARLING

COACH HOUSE BOOKS, TORONTO

first edition

 Canada Council   Conseil des Arts   ONTARIO ARTS COUNCIL   Canadä
for the Arts   du Canada   CONSEIL DES ARTS DE L'ONTARIO
                                     an Ontario government agency
                                     un organisme du gouvernement de l'Ontario

Published with the generous assistance of the Canada Council for the Arts and
the Ontario Arts Council. Coach House Books also acknowledges the support
of the Government of Canada through the Canada Book Fund and the Government of Ontario through the Ontario Book Publishing Tax Credit.

LIBRARY AND ARCHIVES CANADA CATALOGUING IN PUBLICATION

Title: Not anywhere, just not / by Ken Sparling.
Names: Sparling, Ken, author.
Identifiers: Canadiana (print) 20220477191 | Canadiana (ebook) 20220477221 |
ISBN 9781552454640 (softcover) | ISBN 9781770567610 (EPUB) | ISBN 9781770567627
(PDF)
Subjects: LCGFT: Novels.
Classification: LCC PS8587.P223 N68 2023 | DDC C813/.54—dc23

Not Anywhere, Just Not is available as an ebook: ISBN 978 1 77056 761 0 (EPUB); ISBN
978 1 77056 762 7 (PDF)

PART 1

SEPTEMBER

The boy disappears in September, the month he was born, the month he and the girl got married. One minute he's down in the basement sorting through his books, the next he's gone, his books stacked in a dozen piles at the base of the overflowing bookshelves that line the back of the unfinished rec room.

The girl stands by the back window watching a black squirrel dig about in the garden. A red squirrel sits in a tree picking at the fur on its stomach with its teeth. The two squirrels don't seem to notice each other. The girl watches as the black squirrel pulls something out of the ground. The red squirrel seems briefly interested in what the black squirrel has unearthed, but then it scampers away through the trees and disappears as if nothing has happened. A moment later, the black squirrel runs off too. The girl goes to the fridge to try to find something to make for dinner. She pulls out a head of lettuce. She tries to think how long it's been there. She takes it out of the plastic bag. The outside leaves are black and wet. She pulls them off, dumps them in the compost. Washes her hands. Rinses the head of lettuce. Sets it by the sink. Goes back over to the window and looks out. The car is in the driveway. She thinks the boy must have gone for a walk. There was something she wanted to tell him. She tries to remember what it was.

The girl dreams that she's standing by the kitchen counter. The boy is at the stove, wooden spoon in hand. He's in the midst of telling the girl something, but the girl feels like she's arrived too late to understand. She's missed too much. 'Because of the supreme difficulty of remaining indifferent to the smells that invade my being when I'm cooking,' says the boy, 'I cannot ever quite achieve the level of expertise that would allow me to help something come into existence through the parsing of ingredients.' He swings the wooden spoon around as he talks, like he's conducting an orchestra. 'The combination of ingredients is not the bottom line,' he tells the girl. 'Rather, it is that sudden moment when you brush aside half of what you intended to include that finally determines the outcome of your efforts.' *Oh*, the girl thinks, *the boy must be working on his cookbook.* She moves into the kitchen tentatively. The boy is intent on his pot, adding ingredients, stirring. The girl gets up close and looks over the boy's shoulder into the pot. She can't tell what she is looking at. 'Our recipes bring us that much closer together,' the boy says, dropping a pinch of something into the pot. It feels to the girl as though the boy is talking not to her, but to the pot of liquid boiling on the stove. The steam from the pot rises, as though in answer to what the boy is saying, carrying an aroma the girl can't place. She still can't figure out what's in the pot. 'What's that smell?' she asks the boy. 'Our recipes bring us that much closer to the utter indifference we are already on our way to embracing,' the boy says, shrugging. The girl reaches past the boy and taps the tip of her finger to the roiling liquid. She brings her finger to her nose. She recognizes the scent now. It's the smell of escape.

The girl wakes up and sits on the edge of the bed, rubbing her face, trying to bring herself back to life. She checks the clock. It's 3:00 a.m. *Where is the boy?*

The girl remembers when God was living in their garage. It made her nervous knowing God was down there, directly beneath her, while she sat in the kitchen eating or stood at the sink doing dishes. For many weeks, she'd been afraid when the boy left the house and she was stuck home alone with God. Now she wishes God were still there so she could go down and ask her what she's done with the boy.

The very first time the boy saw the girl, it was at a dance club north of town. The club was really just a restaurant where they cleared away the tables on Saturday nights to make a dance floor. They played disco music and flashed strobe lights at a mirror ball that spun from the ceiling in the middle of the dining room. The boy went there with his friends every weekend to dance and meet girls. When he saw the girl, she was walking away from him across the dance floor with some friends, laughing and talking. She had on a blue terry cloth tube top. When a song the boy liked came on, he headed across the room toward the girl to ask her to dance.

The girl feels like she should do something, maybe go out and look for the boy – like he might be somewhere in the neighbourhood, just a little bit lost, unable to find his way back home, and if she were to just walk over to the park and talk to the people there, she might be able to track him down. Like as if the cat got out and she needed to put up some posters on hydro poles.

The piles of books in the basement are like little towers. Like a little city of ruins spread out in the lee of the bookshelves. There are a bewildering number of them, considering how small the basement is. *They're like little statues,* thinks the girl, *like the boy in different poses.* She feels that the boy might be in there somewhere, hiding among the books. Like one of those villains who makes a thousand copies of themself so you can't figure out which one is real. The girl listens to the furnace, surprised how loud it sounds. She can smell it, a faint chemical burning. She picks up one of the books, opens it. Leafs through the pages. It's full of the boy's messy scrawl. Pages and pages, some with big X's through them, others with red ink in the margins. She looks down at the piles. The books all have the same dark blue cover. The towers aren't made of books, the girl realizes. They're the boy's journals. She looks up from the piles. Interspersed among the actual books on the bookshelves are more of the boy's blue-spined journals. *There must be hundreds of them,* thinks the girl. She puts the journal back on the pile she got it from and the tower totters, like it might collapse. The girl feels woozy. She drops to the floor. Sometime later, she looks up. *How long have I been here?* she thinks. She must have fallen asleep. *Where is the boy?* She scoops up one of the journals and opens it, as if she might find him in there.

Dick was ten. He was sitting with his back against the chain-link fence that bordered the empty lot next to the little plaza at the end of his street. The little girl he thought he was in love with was beside him, her bare legs sticking straight out of her pink dress. She had ribbons in her hair. Dick held his hand out, palm open, showing the little girl his coins. There were eight: three nickels, four pennies, and a quarter. 'It was my birthday yesterday,' he said. The little girl smiled at Dick. 'I'm nine,' she said. A tall droopy pine tree rose up beside the fence, eclipsing the sky behind them. 'I'm going to get some candy at the store,' Dick said. 'You want to come?'

The little girl shook her head, making her pigtails swing. 'I'm not allowed,' she said. Dick shrugged and stood up. He stuck his money in the pocket of his shorts. His knees were smudged with dirt. He looked back over his shoulder as he rode his bike across the plaza parking lot. That was the last time Dick ever saw the little girl he thought he was in love with.

When the garage door went up, the light hurt God's eyes. She held up her arm. Her face was pale. She'd been staying in the garage for a week now. The boy didn't want her to leave. But the girl did. 'I don't like having her down there,' she told the boy. 'It's only temporary,' said the boy. 'I can feel her down there all the time,' said the girl. 'Plus, we have no place to put our car.'

'There's no way to describe it. No way to say where I was. I wasn't anywhere. I just wasn't.' The girl is watching an interview with a man who has returned after disappearing a year ago. The man is young, much younger than the boy, who, wherever he is, will turn sixty in a couple days. The young man is facing the camera. The interviewer is out of sight, presumably behind the camera. When he asks a question, his voice sounds hollow. It's impossible most of the time to tell what he's saying. The girl is sitting up in bed, her laptop on her lap. There is a cup of coffee on the bedside table with steam rising from it. The window is a little bit open. The air coming into the bedroom is cool and fresh. The cat lifts its nose, then lifts it again and again in little increments, until its head is arched back and its nose is pointing almost straight up at the ceiling. The girl hears a car out in the street. She starts to get up and go to the window to see if it's the boy pulling into the driveway, but then she remembers the car is already there. The boy didn't take it. She bites her lip and looks back at the laptop. 'Look,' says the man being interviewed, 'there's no way to explain this, really. To you, to my family and friends, to everyone who knew me, I just disappeared. One day I was there, the next I was gone. No one knew where I was.' He pushes his face toward the camera. The interviewer says something unintelligible. 'It was exactly the same for me,' says the young man. He looks down, then back up at the camera. 'You see what I'm trying to say here?' he asks. 'It was as though I was with the family, mourning my own disappearance. From my perspective, it was the same as from their perspective. I was gone to myself. Disappeared. I was nowhere.' He shrugs.

The flowers in the front garden are dying. The girl should get out there and clean things up, get ready for winter. But she wants to wait till the boy is back to help her. *Where the hell is he?* she thinks. This is like some kind of bad dream. Or like a painting she's made with inferior paint, and now it's all decaying. She closes her eyes, then opens them and closes the blinds, as though she can make this all go away by not looking. She sits down at the kitchen table. She moves her glass of water off the placemat and sets it on top of a napkin. She picks up the placemat with both hands, keeping it horizontal as she ferries it to the sink, cradling it as if it's some kind of fragile creature she might injure or kill if she isn't careful enough. She holds it over the sink, letting go with one hand, shaking it gently to get the crumbs off. Then she carries it back over to the table and sets it in its place, smoothing it out with the palms of her hands. She moves the glass of water from the napkin back onto the placemat, then slides it to the upper left corner. She sits back to look at what she's done.

'I dreamed I found a flower that had fallen off a plant out front and I brought it in and put it in a bowl of water on the table by your placemat.' The boy was sitting up in bed. This was in the middle of the night in August, right before he disappeared. 'Was it one of those pink flowers?' asked the girl. She stared down at the place where her hands would have been if it weren't too dark to see them. 'No,' said the boy, 'it was shaped like one of those pink ones, but it wasn't pink.' They sat in silence. 'Was it red?' the girl asked. 'I think so,' said the boy. 'Which bowl did you put it in?' asked the girl. 'One of the cereal bowls,' said the boy. The girl said nothing. 'Maybe I should have put it in a nicer bowl,' said the boy. The girl giggled. 'It was a dream, silly. You can't make choices in a dream.'

The girl goes online and gets the number for the local police station. She feels nervous as she punches the number into her phone. *I probably won't be able to get through*, she thinks. *With all these people disappearing, there must be thousands of people calling the police.* She tries to slow her breath. *At least it's a place to start*, she thinks. *I have to start somewhere.* She rehearses what she will say when someone picks up the phone. She's afraid they will ask if the boy hasn't just left her, got sick of her, given up on her. She knows in her heart this could never be. The boy is so committed to her that at times it terrifies her. But the police won't know that. *He would lick my boots if I asked him*, she plans to tell whoever it is who answers the phone. She imagines the boy on the floor, under the kitchen table, licking her boots. Then he is taking her boots off and licking her feet. A recorded message comes on. They are experiencing staff shortages. There are not enough of them left to answer the phones. This isn't what the message says, exactly, but this is what the girl understands. *Of course*, she thinks, *the police must be disappearing, too.* 'If this is an emergency,' the message says, 'call 911. If you are calling about a missing person who is a citizen of Canada, please visit www.disappeared.ca. If you are calling about a missing person who is not a Canadian citizen, please visit www.disappeared.un.' The girl ends the call. She looks under the table, where the cat is sitting, busily licking away at the moisturizing cream she put on her feet this morning. 'You're disgusting,' says the girl. The cat looks at the girl for a moment, then goes back to licking her feet.

Every place in the house where the boy isn't is the place where he disappeared, thinks the girl. She imagines the boy floating up through the ceiling. The house is so quiet. The cat wanders past, headed for another part of the house. The girl follows it. *Maybe it knows where the boy went*, she thinks. *Maybe it saw what happened.*

Another time the boy was sitting on the orange rug in the basement holding a book in each of his hands. The girl was standing behind him. 'This is too hard,' said the boy. 'Then don't do it,' said the girl. 'Don't you want me to get rid of some of these books?' asked the boy. 'Yes,' said the girl. 'But who cares what I want? I want a lot of things.' The boy waved the two books he was holding in the air. 'Which one do you think I should get rid of?' he asked. The girl shrugged. 'How should I know? I've never even read any of your books.' She shifted her weight from one foot to the other, jutting her right hip out. 'Your books are stupid,' she said. The boy laughed. 'That's true,' he said. 'Yet for some reason I like them.' 'That's because you're stupid,' said the girl.

The boy laughed again. 'That's true, too,' he said. He looked from one book to the other. 'What I really need,' he said, 'is a rule for when to keep a book and when to get rid of it.' 'What if,' said the girl, 'the book is orange, you get rid of it?' 'You think I should get rid of the orange one?' asked the boy. 'I think you should stop trying to make stupid rules,' said the girl. 'But seriously,' said the boy, 'which of these books do you think I should get rid of?' The girl looked at the books for a moment. 'The green one,' she said. The boy looked at the book in his left hand. He sighed. 'Okay,' he said. He tossed the book into a box that was sitting on the floor at the base of the bookshelves. He looked at the book in his right hand. It was the orange one. 'I should just get rid of them all,' he said. He tossed the orange book into the box. 'I'll just get rid of all of them,' he said again. 'You don't have to,' said the girl. 'You don't have to get rid of any of them.' The boy turned and looked at the girl. 'I've got to get rid of some of them,' he said. 'I'm never going to be able to read them all. Even if I live to be a hundred.' The girl said nothing. 'And anyway,' said the boy, 'what happens if I disappear?' The girl breathed out through her nose. 'You're not going to disappear,' she said. 'Neither of us is going to disappear.' The boy picked up two more books. 'You don't know that,' he said. He looked at the books. 'Eventually one of us is going to leave,' he said. 'Even if neither of us disappears, one of us is going to die someday.' He tossed both the books he was holding into the box with the other two. 'And whoever's left,' he said, 'will be alone.' He shook his head. 'I don't want to leave you all alone with this mess.' The girl shifted her weight back to her left foot. 'I'd rather you didn't leave me,' she said, 'but if I have to be alone, I'd rather be alone with your mess than with nothing at all.'

The girl stands on the ugly orange throw rug that the boy has laid by the bookshelves so he doesn't have to sit on the concrete floor as he sorts through his books. The rug is a spiral affair that looks like it was made by one of those knitting spools that vomit out tubes of wool. *Forget the books, you dummy*, thinks the girl. *If you wanted to get rid of something, why didn't you just toss this ugly fucking rug.* She laughs in a way that hurts, then sits down on the floor, legs crossed, elbows on her knees. She runs her hands over the rug. She's never looked at it this closely. Somehow it doesn't look so bad from here, even though it smells like disgust and feels like sitting on corrugated steel. She picks up one of the journals and starts to read.

A guy once said to Dick, 'Is there any pop left in the machine?' It was a guy Dick didn't know. The guy was in some kind of uniform that didn't quite fit. They were in a building full of shops. People streamed by with bags in their hands. It was noisy, like a gymnasium. 'Hey there, old man,' said the guy in the uniform, 'if it isn't too much trouble, I'd like to buy a pop.' Dick looked at the uniformed guy. 'Step aside, old man,' the guy said when Dick didn't show any signs of moving. In his mind, Dick was back at the variety store, buying a grape pop for the little girl he hadn't seen since he was ten. The uniformed guy stepped forward, nudging Dick aside, then reaching toward the machine. There was the clink of a coin dropping into the pop machine. Then the clunk of a can landing in the dispenser. The uniformed guy bent over with a grunt and retrieved the pop. It was a Tahiti Treat.

On their first date, the boy and the girl went to the Dairy Queen. The boy picked up the girl in his mom's Plymouth Valiant. 'My aunt had one of these Valiants,' the girl told the boy. 'They last forever.' They drove past Crosby Avenue. 'This car even smells like my aunt,' said the girl. The boy saw some of his friends walking along the sidewalk talking and laughing. 'Duck down,' he told the girl. He pushed her head down under the dashboard. Thirty years later, when the girl reminded the boy that he did this, the boy told her: 'I was very young. And anyway, we were only pretending. It wouldn't have been bad if anyone saw us together, but we pretended it would ruin our reputations. I thought it would be funny.' 'Well, it wasn't funny,' said the girl. She looked at her fingernails. 'What I wanted to know,' she said, looking back up at the boy, 'was where was the Beetle? I thought you were going to pick me up in the Beetle. That was one of the things I liked about you. You were funny, when we danced you didn't try to touch my bum, and you drove a Volkswagen Beetle.' The boy remembered how hard it had been not to touch the girl's bum when they were dancing. 'What I miss most about the Valiant,' he said, 'was the bench seat. You don't get those in cars anymore.'

The boy might just be lost, thinks the girl. This immediately seems stupid, but it also makes a sort of sense. The boy has always seemed a bit lost. *I should try to find him,* thinks the girl. She opens the boy's laptop, like she might find him inside. The wallpaper is a picture of the cat looking like an idiot. The boy used to keep a picture of the girl looking like an idiot as his wallpaper, but the girl made him change it. She doesn't know what to type into the search box. Her fingers hover over the keyboard for a long moment. *Does everyone who disappears come back,* she types quickly. Then just as quickly she holds down the backspace key, causing the cursor to swallow up the letters she has typed, like a shark taking out a row of scuba divers. The girl gets this sudden premonition that the boy is back, that she should go to the front door right now and open it instead of sitting here staring at his computer. She pulls down the lid of the laptop. She sits for a moment, hating her uncertainty more than anything. Then she opens the laptop again and waits for it to blink back to life. She wants the boy to come back now. Or to never come back. She hates herself for having this thought. She closes the laptop with as much finality as she can muster, then goes down to the kitchen to make some coffee.

'I'm not looking for the boy,' says the girl, glancing up from a journal she has found in the boy's bedside table. 'I never was.' The cat looks at her for a moment, then lies back and yawns, stretching its body to the point where it quivers. Then it stays still with its head upside down, its front paws stretching straight up, like it's some kind of criminal surrendering to the cops. 'I'm telling you the truth here,' says the girl. The cat blinks. 'It was completely the other way around,' she says. 'The boy came looking for me.' She scratches the cat under its chin. 'And for some reason I can't quite fathom,' she says, 'I never tried to get away.'

OCTOBER

'This is a story about Dick,' the boy told the girl. 'I hate that name,' said the girl. She looked down at her hair hanging by her shoulder. 'Can't you call him something else?' The boy blinked. 'His name is Dick,' he said. 'But you made that up, right?' said the girl. 'This is just a story, right?' she asked. 'It isn't about a real person.' 'Right,' said the boy. 'Then you could just change his name,' said the girl. The boy looked troubled. 'I can't just change the guy's name because you don't like it,' he said. 'Why not?' asked the girl. The boy tried to think of a reason. What he wanted to tell the girl was really a lie. It did feel sometimes like things happened in his head outside of his control. But at any time, if he was honest with himself, he could change those things. Couldn't he? He could certainly change Dick's name. 'Why don't I tell you this story,' he said after a moment. 'Maybe after you've heard it, you'll think Dick is perfect for this guy.' The girl looked dubious. 'Maybe,' she said. She squinched her cheeks. 'Okay,' she said. 'Tell it.' 'Dick,' the boy began, but before he got anywhere the girl stuck her finger in her throat to mime gagging. 'Very funny,' said the boy. He waited for the girl to finish fake throwing up, then repeated: 'Dick … ' He paused to make sure the girl was truly finished. 'Dick,' he said once more, 'turned sideways on the couch and stretched his long legs out along the empty space beside him.' The boy watched the girl. She seemed to be done with the clowning around. 'Dick scooched down so that his head was on the armrest. He tried to focus on what was going on on TV, but it was hopeless. He scooched down a little more into the mushy cushions on the aging couch and closed his eyes. *It's a news broadcast,* Dick realized as he was drifting off to sleep.' 'If this is just another story about you,' said the girl, 'I strongly protest you calling yourself Dick.' 'It's not about me,' said the boy, and then he carried on with the story before the girl could interrupt again. 'The last thing Dick heard before he fell asleep was, "Details about the jailbreak after these words from our sponsor."' The boy stopped. The girl looked at him like he was a little child who kept asking why.

'And then one day I was back.' The guy being interviewed is maybe eighteen with blond hair cropped short, like a guy in the army. 'I hadn't really gone anywhere, though,' he says. 'It was more like a state of mind. Like they changed my state of mind. It was like being on a drug. Some kind of hallucinogenic drug.' The guy looks confused. 'Don't get the wrong idea,' he says, looking straight at the camera. 'I never take drugs.' He seems so serious, like a kid doing a book report. 'But the way I felt while I was gone, that's the way I imagine it might feel to be on drugs.' He grimaces. 'Cripes,' he says, 'I hope I don't start having acid flashbacks.' He's got some sort of southern accent. He looks afraid. The interviewer says something, and same as before, the girl can't make it out. She turns on the captioning. The army guy is nodding, looking pensive. 'I was suddenly nothing,' he says, 'and then a moment later – no, not even a moment later, because being nothing is being nowhere, so when I was suddenly something again it was like I was simultaneously something and nothing and something again. Like it all happened at once.' The guy shrugs. The girl looks away from the screen. Through the crack in the curtains, the sky is blue with fluffy white clouds. The trees look skeletal. The interviewer speaks. The girl looks back at the screen in time to see the caption: 'Did it change you?' The army guy says nothing, just stares into space. 'Have you noticed any lingering effects?' the girl reads. The interviewer sounds like he's asking his questions from inside a tin can. The army guy looks up, presumably at the interviewer. He doesn't move or say anything. *He might be thinking*, thinks the girl, *or he might just have given up.* The image fades and the window on the girl's laptop goes black. There's a tiny curled arrow in the middle of the blackness that the girl can click to see the interview again. A five-second countdown threatens to play another interview. The girl closes the laptop and sets it on the bedside table. She can smell the boy, as though he is there beside her in the bed. *I should wash the sheets*, she thinks.

The girl visits www.disappeared.ca. She navigates through a slew of disclaimers. Eventually she comes to a form that asks for the boy's name, address, date of birth, social insurance number, and the date and circumstances of his disappearance. The girl fills out all the fields that are marked with asterisks, but when she goes to hit the Send button, she hesitates. She wants to include something more. There isn't enough here. *What good can this do?* she wonders. She gets up from the kitchen table. On the way down to the basement, she stops in the front hall. She opens the door. She doesn't know what she's expecting to find. She sees a squirrel skitter down out of a tree, stopping in the middle of the road to sniff at something. She can hear a car pulling away from the stop sign up the road. She closes the door. In the basement, she decides it doesn't matter which journal she picks. Nothing is certain down here. Like falling into a whirling vortex in the middle of the ocean. She bends over the piles. Her hair falls across her face. She pushes it away, grabs a journal, takes it upstairs. In the kitchen, she feels better. Like she's accomplished something, although she has no idea what. She opens the journal to the first page and sets it on the table beside the laptop. In the 'Other Comments' field on the form, she types in the first four sentences from the journal. She reads them over. They constitute a short description of Dick. *God, I hate Dick*, the girl thinks. She hates the government too, she decides. She hits Send.

'Dick's mother went out and started her car.' The boy was reading aloud to the girl. 'She drove to work. At work, she phoned Dick.' The girl interrupted. 'Is that your journal?' she asked, pointing to the book the boy was holding. 'It's Dick's journal,' said the boy. The girl laughed. 'There is no Dick,' she said. 'You just made him up.' 'That's true,' said the boy. He waited. 'Why do you make stuff up?' asked the girl. 'Isn't a journal supposed to be about the person writing it? Like a diary?' 'Maybe,' said the boy. When he didn't elaborate, the girl asked, 'So what *did* Dick say to his mother when she phoned?' 'I don't know,' said the boy. 'Dick didn't write that in his journal.' The girl snorted. 'So what did Dick write?' she asked. 'That's what I'm trying to tell you here,' said the boy. He went back to reading from the journal: 'After work, Dick's mother drove home. She turned on the TV. Later, she turned off the TV and went to bed. She slept. Woke. Slept some more. Sometime after midnight, she got up to pee. She peed, then went back to bed. She lay on her back with her eyes open.' 'Is this about your mother?' asked the girl. 'No,' said the boy. 'I already told you, this isn't about me.' 'Is it about my mother?' asked the girl. 'No,' said the boy, more forcefully. 'This is just some mother I made up. I wanted Dick to have a mother.' The girl didn't really believe this. She was pretty sure every story the boy told was about himself, no matter how much he tried to hide the fact. But she stayed quiet, sitting beside the boy, thinking about their respective mothers, until she felt something itch on her leg, and by the time she finished scratching it she'd forgotten everything they had ever said about Dick, or about mothers, or about anything other than what they were seeing as they stood together looking out the living room window.

'I was born in the barn,' said the boy. 'You never had a barn,' said the girl. The boy went on as though he hadn't heard her. 'Mother had just come out to milk the cows when she felt me coming,' he said. The girl giggled. 'Horses blew steam,' said the boy, 'and they stamped. They made that noise horses make with their lips.' The girl made the horse noise. She butted the boy's chest with her head. She clawed at the air in front of her as if she were a horse dancing around on its hind legs, getting ready to come down and crush the chest of the bastard who had been whipping her all these years. The boy fell backwards onto the couch. Outside, the rain started up, pattering against the window like something at the back of the girl's mind tapping to get back in.

Some days, with the boy gone, the girl feels like she's lost in a snowstorm, even though she is safe inside her kitchen waiting for her coffee to brew. Other days, she ties her bathrobe tighter and goes down to the basement to look at the boy's journals. *I should read them all*, she tells herself one morning after she's got her coffee. She looks up to see the first snowflakes of the winter drifting by the window. *I'll just stay in today,* she thinks, *and read the journals.* She goes down to the basement and picks up a couple, holding one in each hand. *I need to read them in order,* she thinks. But she has no idea what order to put them in. There are no clues in the journals. The boy doesn't date or keep the journals in any particular order. He doesn't keep anything in any sort of order. *What I need is a rule for putting them in order,* thinks the girl. She laughs. She hates the boy's rules. But in a way that kind of makes her love him more. His rules are funny. He's funny. Cute. *But so many rules.* She looks down at the piles of journals. They look like turrets built by someone who couldn't afford to finish the rest of the castle. She feels a strong urge to straighten them, but when she leans over to do so, she gets this terrible feeling that moving them will make it harder for her to find the boy. *I should read all of them,* she thinks again. And again she feels afraid.

'My sunglasses got stolen,' Dick said. He was sitting in the sand at the beach, air warm, water lapping gently behind him. 'I had a yellow plastic bucket,' he said. 'I was going to use it to collect some shells.' Dick's mother was standing beside him. She tipped her head down, stared at him. 'I was going to glue the shells together to make you a present,' said Dick. 'But the bucket got stolen.' Dick shrugged. 'I didn't have any money to buy glue anyway,' he said, causing his mother to laugh like some kind of pull-string toy.

A few weeks after the boy disappears, his laptop issues a series of sharp, undulant tones that repeat over and over. To the girl, it sounds like what you'd hear on a spacecraft if an alien race were trying to contact you with an urgent message from the mother ship.

'You're such a he-man,' said the girl. The boy looked at her to see if she was serious. She looked sort of serious. 'Are you serious?' he asked. She kept looking at him, her eyes bright and shiny. She was making him nervous. 'I'm the opposite of a he-man,' said the boy, laughing in a way that sounded frantic. The girl was wearing a tight red top. He'd never seen it before. It looked like she wasn't wearing a bra. The boy wasn't sure. He was trying not to look. The girl slipped her arms around the boy, pushed herself against him. 'Maybe you're right,' she whispered. 'Or maybe you're right,' said the boy, his face disappearing into the girl's hair.

The girl goes to her inbox. She finds the 'Do Not Reply' email she got from the government after she sent the form. She wants to reply. She knows her reply will be lost. It will disappear, like the boy. She rereads the email. *This is stupid*, she thinks. She deletes the email. She closes the laptop and gets up to make herself a coffee. While the coffee brews, she makes a piece of toast. She puts the toast on a plate and butters it. She gets her coffee and adds cream. She brings everything back to the table and reopens the laptop. She finds the 'Do Not Reply' email in her trash and moves it back to the inbox. She rereads it for the umpteenth time, then hits the Reply button. 'Dear Sir,' she begins. But what if someone actually reads her email? What if it's a woman and she's offended at being called 'Sir'? The girl backspaces over 'Dear Sir.' She replaces it with: 'To whom it may concern.' But then she doesn't know what else to write. *Have you found my boy?* This seems so dumb it makes her do that thing she's been doing so much lately, which isn't really laughing but isn't really crying either. It's a new emotion, one she never knew until the boy was gone. It isn't exactly confusion, because confusion isn't an emotion as far as the girl is concerned, it's a lack of emotion. Maybe that's what she's feeling: nothing.

In the bathroom mirror, the girl's face looks empty. She goes to the kitchen. The cat follows. The girl opens the pantry, gets out a can of cat food. It's the last one. *I'll have to go to the grocery store,* she thinks. This scares her. The boy always did the shopping. *I'll just get the cat some food and come straight home,* she tells herself. *I'll get a lot of cat food. I'll get us both a lot of food. And toilet paper. And maybe some cinnamon for my oatmeal. If I get enough, I won't have to go back until all this is over.* At the grocery store, everyone is moving in the same direction. The girl doubles back. Her buggy looks empty. She's got the cinnamon, but she can't remember what else she wanted to get. She stands still at the back of the store. *Just get the cat food,* she thinks, *then get out.* The fluorescent lights make her tired. She's cold. She smells meat. She doesn't know what aisle the cat food is in. She sees a woman stacking pop on a shelf. She asks where the cat food is. The woman looks at the girl. 'I don't work here,' she says. The girl sees the Pepsi logo on her blouse. 'Sorry,' she says. In the end, the girl grabs sixteen cases of tuna. *We can both eat this,* she thinks. She tries to decide what else to get. All she has so far is the cinnamon, a carton of milk, and all that tuna. *I should have made a list,* she thinks, heading to the checkout. The man working the cash eyeballs the girl after she's loaded her items onto the belt. 'Eat a lot of tuna, do you?' he asks. 'Some of it's for my cat,' says the girl. After she's paid, she rushes out of the store, loads the tuna into her trunk, and closes herself into the car before anyone else can say anything to her.

As far as the girl could tell, the story the boy was reading to her was about leaves. Dick was in it, of course, but the main characters of the story seemed to be leaves falling out of trees. The boy stopped reading and looked at the girl. She seemed to be in some sort of distress.

The girl goes downstairs to look at the boy's shoes. He has three pairs sitting on the little shoe rack in the basement hallway. She picks up his running shoes. *What shoes was he wearing when he disappeared?* she wonders. He almost always wore his running shoes. She feels like this must mean something. She pictures the boy on another planet, Mars maybe, standing on the dusty surface in just his socks. She takes the shoes into the rec room and sets them down among the piles of journals. She steps back. It's like some kind of performance art. She imagines the boy standing there, invisible, wearing only his shoes. She pictures a ghostly version of the boy, his body transparent, his old wrinkled penis hanging between his legs. Sometimes, in the right light, it looked sort of cute. Most of the time, though, it looked like some kind of hairy little one-eyed monster, rising up blind in its efforts to find her.

On a Friday morning in late October, the girl sees the boy riding his bicycle. He's hunkered down close to the handlebars and it looks as though he doesn't know how to ride a bike at all, which is ridiculous, because he's been riding a bike since he was four. The girl is in her car, driving in the opposite direction on the other side of the road, but the way the boy is weaving around on his bike, there is the very real possibility that he is going to crash into her. The road is clear of snow, but there are wet patches, and the girl is afraid the boy is going to hit some ice. She can see his breath trailing out behind him. She slows the car. She doesn't think the boy is even going to see her. She clutches the wheel. Glances in the rear-view mirror. Maybe she should just stop the car, pull over. Her foot hovers between gas and brake. The boy seems to be focusing solely on the front wheel of his bike. At the last minute he swerves in front of the girl's car and she hits the brake. The boy comes up along the passenger side of the car. He looks up and sees the girl through the passenger window as he goes by in the opposite direction. He gets this crazy grin on his face and lifts his hand to wave. It isn't the boy. It's just some random guy. He doesn't even look that much like the boy. The guy stands up on his pedals and turns to look back at the girl as he continues wobbling away along the wrong side of the road. The girl realizes she's sitting stopped in the middle of the road. She checks her mirror and pulls away. When she looks again, the random guy is in her rear-view mirror, lying on the snow at the side of the road, his bicycle teetering on the curb, front wheel still spinning. Further along, the girl stops at a red light. She looks in her rear-view mirror again. The guy and his bicycle are gone. For a moment the girl wonders if she's imagined the whole thing. As soon as she gets a chance, she turns the car onto a side street and pulls over to the curb. She shuts off the car. She thinks about walking back to check on the guy and his bike, but she can't even locate the real boy, so how's she going to find this random guy who seems now to have also disappeared?

The boy came up the driveway at five forty-five with his plastic bag. It was already dark. The driveway glittered in the light from the moon. In the boy's plastic bag was the Tupperware that the girl had packed him for lunch that day. All the lights in the house seemed to be on. The man who lived next door stopped the boy at the end of his driveway. He wanted to tell the boy something. The boy stood with his bag of Tupperware hanging by his leg. He could see the girl at the kitchen window. The air was cold. The boy's lips felt numb. When he spoke, the words came out jumbled. The man who lived next door stopped talking. The boy went into his house. There were no empty hangers in the closet. He went upstairs with his coat still on to tell the girl they needed more hangers. He climbed the stairs slowly, wondering what he would find. He never knew what he might find when he came home. There were sounds in the house, but the boy couldn't tell where they were coming from. He found nothing upstairs. He went back down. He counted the coats in the closet, then he divided by two.

It's around one o'clock in the afternoon, the day before Halloween. The girl is drinking coffee at the kitchen table with her eyes closed. The wind outside sounds like the boy's voice whispering something to her from far away. *It's nice to have the boy back here with me*, thinks the girl drowsily, her eyes moving visibly beneath their lids. The boy continues to speak to her in his distant whispery voice. The girl keeps her eyes closed. 'I started walking back to shore,' the boy whispers. 'I was pushing my legs through the water, which came up to just below my knees, but I wanted to go under the water again, so I walked back out to where it was deep enough to dive in.' There is a brief silence as the wind outside dies down, but then picks back up again. 'When I broke the surface, I couldn't touch bottom,' says the boy. 'I had to tread water. I could smell the raw cold of the water just beneath my nose.' The girl hears the boy take a sip of his coffee, and it's then that she remembers he isn't there. Her eyes pop open. 'Where are you?' she whispers. 'Can I come there?' But all she hears is the wind.

NOVEMBER

Nearly two months have passed and the girl hasn't heard anything. She decides she hates the government. Not because they haven't found the boy. But she filled out the form and they haven't done anything. She wants to blame someone, but there's no one to blame. *It's not like the government's a person*, the girl thinks. There's no one person in the government to blame. She could blame the prime minister. But it's not his fault people keep disappearing. At least, she hopes it isn't. She's read some theories. But right now the girl doesn't want to think about the theories. Right now what she really wants is someone to blame, someone to hate, and she doesn't want it to have to be the boy.

The girl looks up at the sky. The clouds are dark and tall. She hopes it won't snow until after she gets home. She walks through the wind as though it were a force field she might penetrate. Maybe the boy is on the other side of this force field, she thinks. She tilts forward into the wind. *It doesn't matter if I never find the boy at all*, she tells herself, *just so long as I go on looking.*

The boy and the girl were standing side by side looking at a sewing table. They were wearing acrylic toques and red mittens. They weren't moving. The sewing table had a lot of drawers and cubbies. 'What would you put in all those cubbies?' asked the boy. 'I'd like to put underwear in some of them,' said the girl. She gave the boy a pointed look. 'Your underwear,' she added. The boy's face looked pinched. 'I mean,' said the girl, 'I want to put unexpected things in the new sewing table. Things

I'd be surprised to see when I opened the drawers. Things you wouldn't normally expect to find in the drawers of a sewing table.' She smiled at whatever it was she was imagining in the drawers of her sewing table. 'Yet,' she said, tilting her head, 'they must be things that I can use for my sewing projects.' She looked directly at the boy now. She was getting wound up, moving her arms around, pointing. 'I could tear the seams out of your underwear and use the fabric to make other things. I could make you a hat. One with ears.' 'Out of my underwear?' asked the boy. 'Sure,' said the girl, 'why not?' 'I don't know if I'd want to wear my underwear on my head,' said the boy. 'I'd wash it first,' said the girl.

The girl is exploring the house, picking up things she's forgotten about. Things the boy gave her. A butterfly fashioned out of copper wire. A clay dog called Stanley. A small wooden box with ivory-coloured inlays on the lid and a scrap of paper inside it with some rules the boy has jotted down. The girl doesn't think of this exploration as a search, exactly. She isn't looking for the boy. Or even for the boy's things. She isn't looking for anything at all. She's just looking. Wandering. The way the boy used to. There's a part of her that is nothing but the boy, she realizes. A part of her that can't do anything but wander. This part of her seems so stark now, so obvious, so available, so unavoidable. And it makes her sad. Or mad. Or crazy. When she comes across one of the boy's journals in some forgotten corner, some locked cupboard, she feels like she is discovering something about herself, about the part of herself that is nothing but the boy.

'I will take off my shoes and feel the earth press into the bottoms of my feet,' Dick tells himself. He is alone in the bright empty room he inhabits in his head. 'I will throw open the gate at the back of morning,' he says, 'and walk over sticks and stones, and put my feet in the river, and feel it stream past my legs. I will put my feet in the air like a monster putting its teeth into the tentacles of the night. I might hold a bird in my hand and pat it. I might push my feet slowly into the ooze at the base of the river's muck.'

The girl drives out of the city and into the country. She comes to an old gas station on a gravel road. She shows the man who pumps her gas the address on the little slip of paper she has in the pocket of her windbreaker. 'That's God's place,' says the man, leaning in through the window of the girl's car to look at the note. He stands up straight, takes off his cap, scratches the top of his bald head. He's got grease on his cheeks. He looks up the road beyond the gas station and points. 'Just go up yonder about two miles, then turn left at the first lane you come to after you pass the Dairy Queen billboard.' The girl nods. The gas station man is about to leave, but the girl stops him. 'God used to live in our garage,' she tells him. The man says nothing, just regards the girl for a time, then puts his cap back on and goes into the station. When the girl is still sitting in her car at the pumps ten minutes later, the gas station guy sticks his head out the door of his shop and calls out to her, 'Is there something else you're in need of, ma'am?' They look at each other. 'No,' says the girl. She goes to close her window, but stops and calls out, 'Thanks.' The gas station guy nods and goes back into his shop. When the girl gets to the lane beyond the Dairy Queen billboard, she turns around and drives back home.

Outside the windows of the train, amid snow-covered trees and icy swamps, two moose watched the train speed by. At the station where the boy and the girl got off, a man beckoned them over to his pickup truck. They squeezed into the cab and sped along a two-lane highway, then lurched onto a gravel road. The boy listened to stones ping the underside of the truck. Twenty minutes later, the man parked in front of a log cabin in a tiny clearing hacked out of the forest. 'You'll have to walk from here,' the man said. 'Just follow the path.' He pointed, then turned and went into the cabin. The door closed with a thud. A heavy silence fell from the trees like something solid. The boy got their things out of the back of the truck. He could see his breath in the still air. 'It smells like pine cones,' said the girl. They headed off along the path. When they reached the little cottage where they were staying for the weekend, a kid was sitting in the snow by the front door with a sandwich in her hand. Her knitted hat had strings dangling from the earflaps. Her cheeks were smeared with the contents of her sandwich. *Peanut butter*, thought the boy, feeling mildly repulsed. He'd been feeling sick since before they got on the train. The kid with the sandwich looked about seven. 'Hi,' she said, grinning through a mouthful of mush. 'Are you the new folks?' The girl nodded. 'You want me to come in and show you around?' the kid asked. As soon as they got inside, the boy set their bags down and crawled into the bed in the corner of the room. The kid took the girl's hand and gave her the tour. One room, with a stove and fridge, along with a couple of cupboards on one side, the bed and a dresser with a mirror over it on the other. In the corner opposite the bed was a little cubicle with the toilet and a shower. There was one window, overlooking the lake, which was frozen over. Under the window was a kitchen sink. 'You can come up to the main house for your meals if you want,' said the kid. 'I have to go now,' she added. 'Don't tell my dad I was here.' When the kid was gone, the girl made some weak tea and brought it over to the boy. She crawled into bed and held the boy in her arms. When the boy woke a while later, the girl was gone. The boy took a sip of the tea, which was cold. He set the teacup on the bedside table, then got out of bed. He went over to the window. He could see the girl out on the frozen lake with the kid. It looked like they were trying to build an igloo. After a while the girl came back in, alone, and sat in a chair by the door. The boy knelt on the floor and slipped off the girl's boots. He inserted his fingers into the necks of her socks and tugged, peeling them down around the girl's heels and past her toes. She lifted her bum as he pulled off her snow pants, then again as he removed her jeans. He eased her legs apart, kissing her knees, then running his hands up the insides of her thighs. 'What were you doing out there with the kid all that time?' he asked. The girl didn't answer. She breathed in and let her head drop back, dangling her hair over the back of the chair. 'You seem to be feeling better,' she murmured, sliding down the chair toward the boy.

The cat is waiting by the door when the girl comes in from the yard. It looks like a statue of a cat. The girl picks it up and carries it to the bedroom. She sets it on the bed and scratches the top of its head. She looks out the window. The sun shines brightly off a thin layer of snow that makes the girl squint. 'The boy is out there somewhere,' she tells the cat. *Or not*, she thinks. She pictures him floating in outer space. She tries to see his face. *He'd be in a spacesuit*, she thinks, *otherwise he couldn't breathe*. She's having trouble breathing herself. She has no energy, no desire, no anything. She crawls into bed, pulls the cat in beside her. Maybe whoever took the boy gave him gills. But space isn't water. *Space gills*, the girl thinks, remembering a movie they watched. What she pictures in the end is the ghostly image of her own face reflected back at her from the glass screen on the front of the boy's helmet. They are drifting together in space, holding on to each other to keep from floating apart. What the girl winds up seeing is her own face superimposed over the boy's face in the glass of their space helmets, which are almost touching. The cat crawls onto the girl's stomach and purrs, stretching out its front paws to reach past her face, as though about to caress her cheeks.

The girl walks toward the park, her boots crunching in the snow. The sky is growing dark, even though it isn't quite dinnertime. A small grey bird lands in a bush in front of someone's house. A blue car goes by with its lights already on. When the girl looks up, she sees the boy striding away from her on the sidewalk. 'Hey,' she calls as she jogs along, trying to catch up. The boy turns. It isn't the boy. It's a different boy. An actual boy. It might have been her boy fifty years ago. This actual boy, who probably isn't even twelve, stands still, his hands dangling at his sides. 'Hi,' he says cheerfully, like he's been expecting her. This startles the girl and she giggles. The actual boy who isn't her boy laughs too. But when the girl's laughter turns a little hysterical, the actual boy turns and walks quickly away.

God kept losing things the boy gave her. 'How do you keep losing everything?' the boy asked. 'Please don't raise your voice with me,' God said. 'I'm sorry,' said the boy, as calmly as he could, 'but how do you keep losing my things? You're living in my garage. You never go anywhere.' 'I understand your frustration,' God said. 'No,' said the boy, 'I don't think you do.' God looked hurt. 'I'm not going to discuss this if you keep yelling at me,' she said. 'I'm not yelling,' said the boy. But he was, and he knew it. And it wasn't God's fault. The boy just wanted God to move out of his garage. Well, actually it was the girl who wanted God to move out of the garage. The boy didn't really care. *But how do you ask God to move out of your garage?*

'I feel like I'm closer to the boy now that he's disappeared,' the girl tells the cat. She scratches the top of its head. 'I'm so close to him,' she says, 'that I'm the same as him.' The cat pushes its nose into the girl's hand. 'It's like it's not him that's gone,' the girl says, 'it's me.' She takes her hand away from the cat's head. 'I'm in this space where there is no one where once there was someone.' The cat lifts its nose. 'That someone could be me, or it could be the boy.' The cat yawns widely, then looks at the girl with its head a little sideways. 'I wish he were here now,' says the girl. 'I would tell him I miss him.' The cat is looking at her, but it has its ears pointed in different directions, like it's just pretending to listen. 'But if he were here, I wouldn't be missing him, would I?' She looks at the cat, then picks it up and puts it over her shoulder, where it hangs like a sack of potatoes waiting to go to the larder.

'I was gone,' says the guy. He's forty, maybe forty-five. 'Really,' he says, 'I swear it.' There's a long pause where the guy – he's some kind of contractor – looks down at his hands. The girl can hear someone, maybe the interviewer, shuffling around in the background. 'But when I came back,' the contractor says, 'no one knew I'd been gone.' He looks down. 'I don't think anyone really believes me when I tell them I disappeared.' He looks back up. 'I mean, they're polite and all. But I don't think they really believe me.' He stops when the interviewer interjects with a question. The girl turns up the volume to try to hear what the interviewer is saying, but then it's too loud when the contractor talks. She thinks about turning on the captions, but she doesn't really care what the interviewer says if he's too stupid to mic himself properly. 'It was dinnertime when I disappeared,' says the contractor. 'The kids were downstairs watching TV. I was washing up. I'd been on-site all day. We're building a house up in the hills north of town.' He gestures with his head, in a northerly direction, the girl presumes. The interviewer interrupts, but the girl still can't make out what he's saying. She's pretty sure he's the same interviewer who talked to the others. The girl has only his voice to go on, but it sounds like the same muffled voice she's heard mumbling in the background in all these videos about people coming back from being gone. The interviewer should really take some kind of course, or elocution lessons, or even just do a YouTube tutorial on how to mic an interview properly, if he's intent on continuing as an interviewer, the girl thinks. The contractor is rubbing the stubble on his face now, shaking his head. 'Nobody even missed me,' he says. 'It felt like I was gone for a long time. Like I'd died and come back. But it was like nobody even cared. I came back downstairs, wondering what day it was, what year even. Selena, my wife, was making pasta. She looked the same as she did when I went up to take my shower. She paid no attention when I came into the kitchen.' The contractor shakes his head. 'Maybe I was gone for only a few minutes,' he says. 'I don't know.' He continues to shake his head slowly. 'Maybe I was never really gone at all.'

'The sun is shining,' says the boy. The girl tries to open her eyes. She knows that when she opens them, the boy won't be there. She knows that she will eventually have to open her eyes. But for now, she decides, she will keep them closed.

The girl was preparing stuffed peppers, chili con carne, grape salad, and a grilled cheese all at the same time when the boy came into the kitchen. 'What are you doing?' the boy asked. 'Cooking,' said the girl. The boy could hear her breathing. 'We need to eat proper meals,' she said after a long silence. The boy tried to think what to say. 'I thought up a new rule today,' he blurted out. The girl reached over and set the oven timer. She had a spatula in one hand and there was some kind of white powder in her hair. 'I don't want any more rules,' she said. She sounded angry. The boy could smell cheese burning. The girl pushed her hands through her hair, making it look even crazier than usual. 'It's a good rule,' said the boy hopefully. The girl had always liked his rules. At least, she always acted like she liked them. 'It will help us get along better,' he said as an afterthought. 'No,' said the girl, setting the spatula down on the counter beside a mixing bowl. Strands of her hair were sticking out from where the ribbon she'd tried to contain them with was slipping off. A piece of her bangs was plastered to her forehead where beads of sweat had broken out. The boy dipped his head. 'But –' he began. 'No,' said the girl. 'No more rules,' she said. 'We're getting along fine.' 'We are?' asked the boy. 'Yes,' said the girl. The boy nodded. 'I thought you liked my rules,' he said. The girl breathed out loudly. 'You're right,' said the boy. 'We don't need any more rules.' The girl picked up the spatula and stuck it into the mixing bowl, keeping her back to the boy. The boy went upstairs and sat on the edge of the bed. 'I probably should have waited till she was in a better mood to tell her about that rule,' he said to the cat. It looked for a moment like that cat was nodding in agreement, but the boy knew that couldn't be right.

The girl can remember some of the words of the tune she and the boy used to sing together. When she tries to sing it, though, it comes out whispery, without substance – no tune, no rhythm. And the words are nonsense. It's like a duet she can conjure in her head but can't sing because she wants to hear both parts and she can't without the boy. It's like remembering the harmonies without hearing them, like a theory of dissonance. The girl's voice emerges unbidden, rises almost hysterically, then settles away, and the sounds she's heard herself making disappear into the ether. And the dissonant memories that follow seem more eerily beautiful than anything she ever actually experienced when the boy was with her.

Dick went out into the front hall to look for his shoes. He was afraid he might not be able to find them. The hall was small, but his shoes never seemed to be where he remembered putting them. He sat down on the bottom step. Mimed taking off his shoes. Tried to think where he would put them now if he had them to put somewhere. He opened the front door, still in his socks. There was rain coming down, falling out of the sky. This seemed unexpected, somehow, but where else would it fall from? I should wear my boots if I'm going out, *Dick thought. He looked over at the shoe mat. His boots were right there. But he needed to find his shoes. Even if he didn't need them now, he was going to need them eventually. And when he did, they needed to be here on the shoe mat. He looked back out the door. A woman was standing in the middle of the street smiling and looking up. The rain was coming down on her face, raining the way rain always does, straight down, except that today it was falling onto the face of this woman. There was a bright light somewhere far across the sky where the clouds were thinning, and out of this light came an angel. She was wearing Dick's shoes.*

When the girl stops reading, she realizes she hasn't been reading at all. It's all a story she's been making up in her head while staring at the words in the boy's journals. Only it turns out it's the boy's head where the story is happening, and the girl is trapped in there with Dick. The girl retrieves the boy's shoes and goes up to the kitchen. She sits quietly in her white nightie, rocking gently back and forth, cradling the shoes and staring out the window, her face lit pale in the morning light.

They were sitting together on the bed in the tiny apartment the girl had moved into when she started university the previous year. The girl was sitting cross-legged behind the boy, who had his legs dangling over the edge of the bed. They could hear water running through the walls. 'Seeing the Mastercard bill makes me sad,' the girl told the boy. 'It's weird the things that make a person sad,' said the boy, turning his head to look at the girl. 'I know,' said the girl. Her eyes looked big. 'The Mastercard bill is just this piece of paper, right?' The boy nodded. 'It comes in the mail once a month.' The boy nodded some more. 'You open the envelope. You take out the bill.' The girl looked at her hands, mimed taking out the bill. 'You pay it.' She shrugged. 'And then you just … ' she searched for words ' … put it in a file some-where.' She shook her head. The boy continued to nod. 'And then one day,' the girl said suddenly, 'out of nowhere,' she looked past the boy, as though trying to see into nowhere, 'you see it there in front of you again, on the counter.' The girl looked stricken. 'It's not the same bill, of course.' She laughed a little. 'It's not the bill you put in that file all those years ago.' The boy watched the girl's face. 'But in a way,' said the girl, 'it's the same bill. It's always the same bill.' The girl slipped her arms up under the boy's, resting her hands on his chest. She could feel the boy breathe. She put her lips on the back of his neck. The boy turned and put his hands low down on the girl's back. He kissed her softly. The girl let her mouth relax, open. She felt the boy pushing her over.

Maybe the boy is right here in the house somewhere, thinks the girl, *and all I have to do is open my eyes to see him.* But her eyes are open. *Maybe if I close them*, she thinks.

The cat follows the girl around the house. When the girl goes out to the backyard to sit in the plastic lounger and read one of the boy's journals, the cat stands on its hind legs, front paws against the screen door, watching the girl. Its face looks blurry through the screen. 'Go away,' says the girl. But the cat stays where it is. The girl feels guilty. The boy would have gotten up to let it out. *I'm so lazy*, thinks the girl. But she knows it isn't laziness. It's something else. Something to do with the boy and his stupid cat. She doesn't want it out here with her. It wants too much from her. *It's a cat*, she thinks. *It doesn't want anything from me.* She clucks her tongue. *It probably wants to be left alone more than I do.* She reads some of the boy's journal, then gets up to go back into the house. She squats down as she opens the door and grabs the cat to keep it from running out into the yard. She has half a mind to let it go. She throws it over her shoulder. 'He's not back there,' she says into its fur. 'You have to stay inside with me.' She goes to the kitchen and sets the cat on the floor. After dinner, they sit together in the living room and the girl tells the cat what she read in the boy's journal that afternoon.

'When you first jump into the deep end of the pool,' says Dick to the woman he is living with, 'there's all that space between you and the bottom of the pool.' Dick is standing at the window, afraid to turn around. 'Well,' he says, 'it's like that whenever I'm alone in a room with you.' The woman is standing behind Dick, her white legs poking out of her dress like twin sticks in a cartoon about talking popsicles. 'Tremulous,' Dick says. 'That's how I feel. It felt the same when I was a kid and I went into the gymnasium at school and no one else was around. It's the kind of space you just can't get used to.'

It was Saturday. The boy and the girl stayed close together all day. They laughed. It was fun. They were happy. At one point, they found themselves laughing together at the same time. It was really fun.

The girl sits alone in the living room. She is suddenly very afraid of the boy, even though he isn't there. *He always seems so empty,* she thinks. She looks out the window and the light cuts her face in half. There are shadows on one side of the room. 'The truth is,' she says to the cat, 'I am always afraid.' The cat is lying on the rug in the middle of the room, licking one of its front paws. It stops for a moment when the girl speaks, then goes back to licking. 'But this is a different kind of fear,' the girl says. 'Not the ongoing, almost gentle fear I generally feel.' She looks thoughtful, then shakes her head, like some kind of animal just come in from the rain – not a dog or a cat, but something similar, maybe a coyote, or a lynx. 'The boy is wacko,' she says, laughing a mirthless little laugh. 'We both know that.' She looks to the cat for confirmation. The cat is trailing the edge of its paw across the top of its head, flattening its ear, pink side up, as it does. The girl watches the ear get flattened, then pop up again. 'And yet,' she says, still looking directly at the cat, 'for some reason, I've never wanted him to go away.' She laughs a little. 'Well, that's not true. There were plenty of times when I wanted him to go. But I never wanted him to leave me. I always wanted him to come back.' She shakes her head again, no longer looking at the cat, no longer looking at anything. 'I don't know why that is,' she says with genuine befuddlement. 'I always found myself treading carefully around him, when, in reality, I should have stomped on him long ago like an insect.'

It's nearly December when a guy from the government calls. He asks the girl to quote her case number. She has it on a piece of paper stuck to the fridge. She quotes it, and the government guy quotes it back. 'I just need to verify the information you entered online,' he says. After he's done confirming everything, he asks the girl if she has any questions. 'Did you read the stuff about Dick?' the girl asks. There's a long silence. Then the government guy says, 'Oh yeah, I see it here. You mean the stuff in the "Other Comments" field.' 'Yes,' says the girl. There's another silence, this one not quite so long. 'Okay, I've read it,' says the government guy. More silence. 'And?' asks the girl. 'And … well … it's interesting.' 'You think?' asks the girl. 'To tell the truth,' says the government guy, 'I'm not sure what to think.' The girl laughs. 'That makes two of us,' she says. She decides maybe she doesn't hate the government so much. Well, anyway, she doesn't hate this guy. She kind of likes this guy. His voice is nice. He sounds young. He's not actually the government, she knows, but he's as close to the government as she'll ever come. 'Do you think he'll come back?' asks the girl. 'What exactly is being done about all these people disappearing?' The government guy explains, very patiently, that he's just a volunteer collecting information and that he has no idea what exactly is being done. 'You probably know just as much as I do,' he says. 'Probably more,' he adds, laughing. 'The only thing I really know is that the government is collecting information. I mean, of course I know that, that's what I'm doing. But that's about it.' The girl says nothing. 'Are you there?' the government guy asks. The girl doesn't know what to say. She wants to keep this guy on the phone. There's no one but him to talk to about the boy. Except the cat. But she's sick of talking to the cat. 'Hello?' says the government guy. 'If you're still there, I just want to say that I'm sorry I can't be of more help, but I'm trying to do my part.' He waits, then says, 'I like the stuff about Dick. Yours is the best form I've read so far.' Both he and the girl are silent for a moment, then the government guy says: 'I have to go now. Again, I'm sorry for your loss.' He hangs up the phone, leaving the girl to wonder what he means by 'loss.'

The boy buttered a piece of toast. He brought it to the girl. The girl was sitting at the table looking down at her fingers, which looked sewn onto her hands. 'The psychic was wearing really nice cufflinks,' she said. 'Did you take a picture?' asked the boy. 'No,' said the girl. 'I asked, but she's one of those ones who believes a camera steals your soul.' 'That's true,' said the boy. 'I also believe that.' 'But you let people take your picture all the time,' said the girl. The boy laughed. 'I figure my soul is a lost cause anyway,' he said, 'so there's no use pissing people off.' He looked away from the girl, then back. 'It seems to offend people when you won't let them take your picture,' he said. 'The psychic said the lines on my face were hard to read,' said the girl. 'That's her specialty,' she added, 'reading the lines on a person's face.' 'Not the lines on your hands?' asked the boy. 'No,' said the girl. 'She says that's nonsense. She says the lines on a person's face are like a road map. But mine were hard to read. She said that the little scar on my forehead was a point of no return. At first she thought it was a point of departure, but then, after talking to me for a while, she realized it was a point of no return.' 'You have a scar on your forehead?' asked the boy. 'Yes,' said the girl, 'it's very small.' 'I never knew you had a scar,' said the boy. The girl shifted her head around so that she was facing the boy. 'I thought you might have noticed it one of those times that you were licking my face,' she said, with a funny little look that made the boy giggle. He moved a little closer to the girl. The girl pulled her hair back and pushed her forehead forward. She put her finger near where she remembered seeing the little scar when she looked at it in the mirror. The boy leaned in closer. Then he darted his head forward quick and licked the girl's forehead. 'Blech,' said the girl. She drove her fists into the boy's stomach. 'Gross,' she said. She wiped her forehead with the back of her sleeve. The boy lunged at her with his tongue sticking out. 'Get away, you pig!' she screeched. She pummelled the boy with her fists. When the boy put his tongue back inside his mouth, the girl watched him warily for a moment, then sat down at the table to eat her toast.

Every place in the house where the girl thinks about the boy is a place where he is now that he isn't. The place where he actually was when he was was never actually the place where he actually was. When he and the girl crossed paths somewhere in the house – like when they both came from wherever they'd been and started to go to wherever it was they were going and wherever it was they were going happened to be the same place, like the bathroom, for example, to brush their teeth at night, or when they both wanted to get a cup of coffee in the morning and they found themselves standing in the kitchen together waiting for the machine to finish brewing and they talked together about whatever it was they were always talking about together, like why is the cat such an idiot, or look at that bird out the window – the boy seemed to be exactly where he seemed to be. But now that he isn't anywhere at all, the boy is everywhere at once. He's in the bedroom with her when she's getting dressed. He's in the kitchen when she's making coffee. He's in the bathroom with his pants around his ankles, peeing while the girl brushes her teeth. Now that he's gone, the girl can't seem to escape him.

DECEMBER

The girl finds one of the boy's journals under some towels in the linen closet. She's wearing yellow rubber gloves, holding a blue sponge in one hand. She sets down the sponge and picks up the journal. She starts to open it, but then sets it beside the sponge and takes off the gloves. She picks up the journal again and opens it to the first page. She starts to read. Another story about Dick. *It's always Dick,* she thinks. She reads a little more. Then she thinks: *I don't have time for this.* She puts the journal back under the towels where she found it, slips the rubber gloves back on, and picks up the sponge. When she gets to the bathroom, the girl's not sure where to start. Before he disappeared, the boy cleaned the bathrooms. She pictures the boy on his knees beside the tub, scrubbing away. She takes a step or two toward the tub, then stops. It's as though she's afraid to get down beside the boy and crowd him out of the picture. She looks around the bathroom. Her hands are shaking. She rips the rubber gloves off and hurls them, along with the sponge, into the tub. She turns and goes back to the linen closet.

Dick goes into the room at the far end of the house, the one with the large window and the drapes always drawn. In the room, there is a blond woman with bare legs. She's wearing a short white dress made of light that presses against Dick's eyeballs like something painful.

'Close the door,' said the girl. From the hall outside the bathroom, she watched the boy pull down his pants. Without turning, the boy reached around and pushed the door closed. The girl put her head close to the door and listened. She could hear the boy's pee hitting the toilet. She spoke through the door: 'You'd close the stall door if you were doing that in a public washroom, wouldn't you?' she said. 'I pee at the urinal when I'm in a public washroom,' the boy called back cheerfully. 'But not with your pants down around your ankles, right?' asked the girl. The boy just laughed and shook his dinger. Drops of golden pee caught the light before gently pocking the surface of the water in the toilet below.

'It was like I could no longer locate my intention.' The man looks tall and skinny, hunched over a big desk in front of a wall of books. He's wearing round, wire-rimmed glasses, and what's left of his hair sticks out in weird directions. 'It was like I still understood intention,' he tells the camera, 'but intention was just this idea that I was holding on to inside my head.' He purses his lips, like he is trying to whistle. 'I myself was like an idea I was holding on to inside my head,' he says. White letters appear at the bottom of the screen: PROFESSOR SASHA MANDELBAUM, UNIVERSITY OF CALGARY. 'My head was like an idea I was holding on to inside my head,' the professor says. He laughs, looks down at his desk for a moment, then back up at the interviewer. 'That sounds absurd, I know.' He shakes his head and tries again. 'The inside of my head was like an idea I was holding on to inside my head.' He starts to get animated, leans forward over his desk. 'And I wasn't holding on to anything!' he exclaims. 'There was nothing to hold on to … And nothing to hold on to it with.' He looks behind him like the answer might be there in one of his books. 'I could feel myself stretching, going out in all directions.' He turns back to the camera. 'But it was like the core of me stayed in one place, and time was a bicycle pump going up and down to inflate me so that I could touch something beyond what I was, without ever becoming anything more than I was, which at that moment was nothing. I was not even the moment in which I felt myself inflating, again and again, to the size of nothing – which it turns out is bigger than anyone might have imagined.' He looks at the camera and laughs jovially, like he's brought the interview to some sort of jolly conclusion. And it seems for a moment like the interview is over. The girl goes to close the laptop, but then the interviewer says something and the professor goes suddenly serious. 'Now?' he says. 'Well, now I guess I miss it.' His eyes tilt inward. 'I want to go back,' he says.

The girl can't find her keys. She sits down on the front hall steps. Stares at her hands. *Say the boy lost his keys*, she thinks. *Say he looked everywhere for them. Checked his pockets. Checked all his pockets – the pockets in all his jackets and all his pants in all the closets around the house.* Weak winter sun shines through the long skinny window beside the front door, illuminating clumps of dirt and leaves on the rug where the girl's shoes are sitting beside her feet. She smells something she associates with the boy's shoes, but all the boy's shoes are in the basement now, with his books. *Maybe he was wearing his sandals when he disappeared*, she thinks. *I hope it isn't winter where he is.* The girl stands, grabs the railing, and pulls herself up the stairs to the bedroom. She opens the clothes closet. Rifles through the boy's clothes. She finds some wadded-up Kleenex in the back pocket of his blue shorts. She puts it on the bedside table and sits down on the bed. *Say he couldn't find his keys in any of his pockets*, she thinks, *so he went around the house checking all the tables and counters and shelves.* She looks down at the wad of Kleenex. She remembers having her keys with her out in the yard. She gets up again, goes downstairs. The cat shows up and follows her out into the yard. 'Say he couldn't find his keys anywhere,' the girl says to the cat. 'But he went out anyway, locking the door from the inside,' she mimes locking the door, 'thinking I would let him in when he returned.' A bird lands on the back fence and the cat hunkers down to stare at it. 'But then I wasn't here when he came home, so he left again and never came back.' The cat continues to stare at the bird, wiggling its bum. 'But why wouldn't he just wait for me?' says the girl, raising her hands in a shrug and looking at the cat. 'Why wouldn't he keep knocking on the door till I let him in?' The bird lifts off from the fence and shoots over the trees. The cat continues to stare at the place on the fence where the bird was before it disappeared.

The boy and the girl were sitting at the edge of the ditch in front of the girl's house. The girl's parents had left the porch light on, but the boy and the girl stayed out near the road, where the light couldn't reach them. It was like they were in a secret cave. The boy lifted his arm. It floated between them in the dark. He slipped his fingers into the thick, curly hair on the back of the girl's head. He bent forward slightly to try to hear what she was saying. She was speaking very quietly, as though to herself. 'When I was a kid,' she said, 'in the fall my dad used to pile leaves in this ditch and let me jump around in them.' The boy stayed as quiet as he could, trying not to move. 'He'd curse because I'd make such a mess of his leaves and he'd have to come out and rake them all up again.' The boy breathed out slowly. The girl was looking down into the ditch. 'But then I'd dive into the pile again, and

Dad would laugh and shake his head and watch me play.' She sat quietly for a moment, staring into the ditch at her feet. 'Every day after school, I'd mess up his leaves and he'd come out and pile them up again. Then one day at the end of November, the town guys would come in their truck and suck up the leaves with a big hose. And that was it for the leaves.' The girl stopped. She looked at the boy. 'I should go in,' she said, standing. 'It's late.' The boy followed her to the front door and they stood under the porch light looking down at their feet for what seemed like the longest time. The boy put his hands very gently on the girl's arms, and when she didn't pull away, he leaned in close, and when she still didn't pull away, he kissed her. A moment later she was gone, disappeared into the house, leaving the boy alone under the porch light, thinking about the little girl she'd once been, playing in the leaves her father had piled into the ditch so that the men from the town could come along in their vacuum truck and suck them all up.

The girl is picturing the baked potato she put in the fridge last night. She worries that the boy will eat it before she gets a chance. Then she realizes that the boy isn't there to eat it, that her potato is safe, and she feels a sense of relief. She stands up from where she's sitting on the couch, intending to go to the kitchen to get the potato. But then she just stays there, not breathing, as though paralyzed, before collapsing back onto the couch, horrified at the idea that she might have felt any sort of relief about the boy being gone.

Crawling into the storage space under the basement stairs, the girl locates the big box with the Christmas tree and drags it out into the hall. She's not sure how she's going to get it up the stairs by herself, not sure she even wants to put a tree up this year. *I can't stop living,* she tells herself. *Eventually I've got to get on with my life.* The boy used to take the girl up north to a tree farm where they would saw down a real tree, but as they got older, that got too hard, so they started getting their tree from a guy who sold them in the parking lot at the mall. Then a couple years ago in January, the boy came home with a fake tree he got at a Boxing Day sale. With the fake tree, the cat doesn't go as crazy as it used to with a real tree, but it still enjoys knocking ornaments off the lower branches. The girl decides she should put the tree up, if only for the cat. She manages to get the box up to the living room. The cat appears out of nowhere and jumps onto it, purring. When the girl scratches it under its chin, it sticks its nose out, purrs louder, and rolls over onto its side, nearly tumbling off the box. The girl catches it, pushes it back up onto the box, then scrunches its face up in her hands. 'You're a fool,' she says. The cat looks disgusted.

'Do you think that woman at the laundromat today was putting us on?' asked the girl. The boy continued brushing his teeth while he thought about this. 'No,' he said after he'd spit his toothpaste into the sink.

Nights are hard for the girl. But those mornings when she wakes up and can't get out of bed are even worse.

The girl sets her yogurt container down on the floor beside the cat for it to lick out the remains. When the cat lifts its head, it's wearing the yogurt container like a mask.

The girl thinks maybe she never really hated the boy's mess – the stacks of books and journals, the bits of paper everywhere. But there is something she hates. She knows that for sure.

'Don't you want to put something on that?' asked the boy. The girl looked down at her toast. 'Why do you care so much?' she asked. 'You don't even like toast.' 'I don't mind toast,' said the boy. 'I don't want to eat it for every meal like you,' he said, 'but I like it okay.' He pushed some things around in the fridge, then pulled out a jar. 'What about pickles?' he asked. 'You love pickles.' The girl looked at the boy standing by the open fridge, holding the jar of pickles. 'Sure,' she said, 'what the fuck. Give me a couple of pickles.'

'When I came back, everything was gone.' The girl looks up from the laptop to the Christmas tree. Its lights – red, green, blue, yellow – make the living room look a bit like the club where she first met the boy. She's glad she decided to put up the tree. The cat seems happy about it too, sleeping contentedly beneath the tree's branches. If the boy were here, he'd be lying on the floor next to the cat, probably sleeping as well. The guy in the interview the girl is watching looks to be in his early sixties, maybe just a little older than the boy. 'While I was gone, my wife sold the house,' he says, 'and moved to this tiny apartment in the city.' The guy looks down, shaking his head. His hair is long and messy and he's got an unruly white beard, which he grabs now with one of his hands, tipping his chin up toward the camera. 'I don't even have a razor,' he says. 'The old girl threw it out.' He laughs in a way that sounds bitter. 'In the place I went when I disappeared, I didn't need to shave.' He looks a little puzzled. 'I don't even know if I had a beard.' He chuckles. 'It didn't seem to matter one way or the other. Nothing did.' He looks down at the floor, then back up at the camera. 'The old house has been torn down,' he says. 'I had a helluva time tracking the old girl down.' He shakes his head again. 'She's not the same woman she was before I disappeared.' He shrugs. 'What did I expect?' he asks. 'It's been almost three years.' He folds his hands over his stomach. 'She threw out all my stuff, or gave it away.' He shrugs again. 'I had a lot of stuff,' he says. 'We lived in that house for more than thirty years.' He hesitates. 'To tell the truth,' he says, 'it actually feels pretty good to be rid of it all.' He makes a face at the camera. 'I wouldn't have minded keeping a few of my books, though,' he says. 'But I guess that's what the library is for … Still, I had a couple of first editions … ' He tapers off and is quiet for a moment. Then he tells the interviewer: 'Anyway, it isn't so much losing all my stuff. Like I said, I'm mostly glad to be rid of it. It's more the fact that there doesn't seem to be any place for me here.' He looks around, and the girl realizes the interview must be taking place in the wife's apartment. 'I feel like I'm camping out here,' the guy says. 'It's a tiny place.' He gestures outward with his hands, and the girl wishes the interviewer would pan around a bit so she could see the place, but he keeps the camera trained on the bearded guy's face. *Doesn't the guy's wife shave her legs?* the girl thinks. *She must have some razors.* But she might not have any shaving cream, the girl realizes. And maybe she waxes her legs. The guy probably wouldn't want to wax his face. The girl laughs. This whole train of thought is ridiculous, she realizes. The guy could just go out and buy some disposable razors. *Maybe they're so broke they can't afford it*, she thinks, feeling bad about her flippancy. 'I've been sleeping on the couch since I moved in here,' says the bearded guy. 'My wife's bed is so small. The bedroom is so small. We couldn't put a bigger bed in there if we wanted.' The guy looks past the camera to where the interviewer must be sitting. 'You want a beer?' he asks, standing up from the couch where he's been sitting. The interviewer declines, then asks in his distant, mumbly voice if the guy's wife is around. Could he interview her? 'She's at her sister's,' the guy says as he steps out of view. There are some sounds off camera – the fridge opening, the clinking of bottles, the hissing of bottle caps being removed – and then the guy returns with two beers. He reaches past the camera with one of them, and when he sits back down, he's only got the one, which he puts to his lips before tipping his head back. He swallows and says, 'She spends a lot of time at her sister's these days.' He takes another swig. 'She'd never admit it, but I think she'd be happier if I'd just stayed gone.' He scratches the back of his head. 'To tell you the truth,' he says, 'I think I'd be happier too.'

They were sitting in the kitchen, eating cereal, when they heard the garage door go up. A moment later the mail flap on the front door creaked open, then clanked shut. The boy got up from the table. He looked around the corner into the front hall. 'It's an envelope,' he said to the girl. Inside the envelope was a memo from God. It said that they should stop and think before they spoke. The following week, they got another memo, this one stating that they should start saying something. *Please*, the memo said. *You need to talk to each other. You need to share.* Finally, there was a memo stating that the practice of whispering to each other in the bedroom was to stop immediately. The next thing was it started to rain. Not very hard at first. But then harder. It rained harder and harder, until rivulets were running down the road, and skinny waterfalls were falling from the tops of buildings, and it looked like no one was ever going to be able to go outside again without an umbrella and a pair of knee-high rubber boots. 'How does God know that we're whispering in the bedroom?' the girl whispered in the bedroom one night not long after they got the final memo. She had just climbed into the bed beside the boy and pulled the covers up to her chin. They could hear the rain pelting the metal eavestrough. 'Is God sneaking into the house at night while we're in bed?' the girl asked. She sounded alarmed. The boy shook his head. 'She doesn't have to sneak in,' he said. 'She's God.'

The girl keeps discovering the boy's journals all over the house. It's like coming across the boy unexpectedly on a Sunday afternoon when both of them are home, each doing their own thing, but neither knowing exactly what the other is up to. The girl tries to leave the journals where she finds them. *Maybe the boy left them in all these weird places for a reason*, she tells herself. She needs to figure out the reason before she starts moving things around. She doesn't want the boy to come back and find that she's moved all his stuff. *It's still his home*, she thinks. What the girl really wants is to go out onto the front porch, close the door and lock it, then walk away and never return. That way, if the boy comes back he will find all his stuff exactly where he left it. He could have his life back the way it was before he disappeared. And the girl could have her life back too. She wouldn't have to disturb the boy's things, or worry about what to do with them. She could just walk away and leave it all behind. She could leave his journals where they are, piled up on the floor in the basement and in the closets and cupboards and drawers where he's left them. And if she ever regrets walking away, she can come back for a visit, like a tourist at a museum dedicated to the boy.

Dick was sitting in the sand with his back against a log. His mother was sitting beside him. She didn't look the way Dick remembered. It was like he'd never seen her before, like the summer was over and this was the first episode of a new season, and the actor who played Dick's mother was no longer available so they slipped in a new woman to play the part. This woman had red hair, which Dick liked quite a lot.

The boy held up his hand. The girl looked. 'Some of my fingers have hair on the backs of them,' said the boy, 'and some of them don't.' 'Really?' said the girl. 'That seems weird.' The boy held his hand up higher and the girl pulled it close to her face. She examined the knuckles. 'You're right,' she said. 'That's so weird.' She looked down at her own hands. At the backs of her fingers. She twisted her hands slowly about in the air as the boy watched, catching glimpses of the girl through her fingers, like something caught in a cage.

Sometimes when she's drifting through the words in the boy's journals, what the girl feels is love. Or something akin to love. It's a feeling of lightness, almost like surrender, and she gets the urge to sit down and be like a pile of books herself. *Maybe the boy would have loved me more if I were a pile of books*, she thinks. This seems funny and, alone in the basement with the boy's journals, the girl lets out a little hiccup that might or might not be a laugh. When she looks at the boy's journals sitting in stacks in the basement, what she feels sits inside her like a lump. She should be able to excise it, examine it, put it under a microscope. She can sense it there, a physical presence. It isn't fear. And it isn't exhilaration. But it's almost exhilaration, and this seems weird.

Dick was looking at himself in the bathroom mirror. He was so old. He was ancient. His skin looked like cobwebs, his eyes were watery and white, and the bits of hair he had left on the sides of his head stuck out like wires. He leaned in over the sink. He wanted to kiss himself on the cheek, to comfort himself, but he realized at the last minute that the only place a person can kiss their mirror image is on the lips.

The girl sits on the couch with the TV clicker in her hand. She keeps her thumb on the channel button, as though any moment now she might go wild and change things up completely. When a commercial comes on, she goes to click the channel button but realizes it's pointless. She has no idea what's on at any given moment. She thinks about getting off the couch. She feels like there's someplace she needs to go, someplace she needs to be, but she doesn't know where it is or how to get there. She could take a taxi, but she doesn't even know if it's possible to drive there. She might have to fly, or take a boat. *Or maybe I should just change the channel*, she thinks.

The boy came home. He had loaves of bread. He was dressed in his brown duffle coat. He felt warm. *I have to take off my shoes*, he thought. *But first I have to put down these loaves of bread.* He stood in the front hall doing nothing. *I don't want to put the loaves on the floor because the cat will run down here and chew through the plastic. It'll try to eat the loaves of bread.* But there was nowhere else to put the loaves. *I don't want to go up to the kitchen with my shoes on and tramp dirt all over the house. And I can't get my shoes off without putting down the loaves.* Eventually he would put the loaves in the freezer. He just didn't know where to put them now. The girl appeared at the top of the stairs. 'What are we going to do with all that bread?' she asked. The boy looked up. 'Could you take these?' he asked, holding out the bread. 'I need to take off my shoes.' The girl's hair drifted gently about her shoulders like it was thinking of leaving her head. 'But what are we going to do with all these loaves of bread after you've taken off your shoes?' she asked the boy. She looked like she'd just gotten out of bed. She was in her nightie. 'They were on sale,' said the boy, as though this would be enough. The girl said nothing. 'They were practically giving them away,' the boy added after a moment. Still, the girl said nothing. 'I thought we could use them for something that a bunch of loaves of bread weren't necessarily meant to be used for,' said the boy. Coming up with an answer that would satisfy the girl felt like trying to steer a rowboat with one oar. The nose of his argument kept drifting off course. 'I thought maybe we could plug them into something, or toss them up in the air, or roll them somehow, like we were bowling.' The girl thought this sounded fun, but she didn't say anything. She didn't want to encourage the boy.

Eventually, the girl learns to stop and stand still whenever she hears the boy moving around upstairs. If she stays quiet long enough, she can sometimes convince herself that he's actually up there. She can hear him going from the bed to the closet to the bathroom and then back again. *He's brushing his teeth right now,* she tells herself.

If someone you know, someone you love, disappears, how do you know it isn't you who has disappeared? From the boy's perspective, it is the girl who has disappeared. From the boy's perspective, the cat has disappeared too. Everybody has disappeared from the boy's perspective. *It must be lonely*, thinks the girl. *He must miss me*, she tells herself. But it's her that misses him, isn't it? How can she know who misses who if she can't even figure out who has gone missing?

The girl was drinking lemonade when the boy came home with a list scribbled onto a bit of napkin he'd scavenged from Tim Hortons. As soon as he got in the front door, he handed the scrap of napkin to the girl, saying, 'Put this in the folder with the other rules.' The girl looked at it, read some of it. 'These aren't even rules,' she said. 'It's just a list.' She read some more. 'This doesn't even make any sense,' she said. She read one of the items on the list aloud to the boy: 'Paint cat box red,' she read. 'How is that a rule?' The boy looked thoughtful. 'Everything is a rule,' he said eventually, as though putting the matter to rest. But the girl wasn't finished. '*Everything?*' she asked. She looked around. 'Is this a rule?' She picked up her glass of lemonade. She set it back down. 'Are you a rule?' She nodded emphatically at the boy. The boy looked surprised, then thoughtful, then he said, 'Yes, in a way I am a rule.' He looked at the girl. 'And you're a rule too,' he said, nodding back at her. 'Everyone is a rule,' he finished. The girl snorted. 'Maybe I should go upstairs and climb into the file with the rest of your rules,' she said. The boy laughed and took her hand. 'I'll go with you,' he said. 'We can live there happily ever after.' The girl let the boy lead her up the stairs. 'Should we bring the cat?' she asked, looking over her shoulder. 'Is it a rule too?'

It's New Year's Eve. *What's it like to not exist?* The girl is standing under the porch light. The air is cold and clear and the moon is shining down on the houses across the street like God's searchlight. *What's it like to come back from not existing?* The girl almost wants to be among this mysterious group of chosen people who no longer exist, but who might once again exist. It's like these people are being reborn. She wants to be reborn.

JANUARY

The girl comes out of the laundry room and for a moment thinks she sees the boy sitting amid his piles of books on the basement floor. But it's not the boy. It's just more books. 'I need to go to Home Depot,' she says. The boy looks up from the book he has open in his lap. *He's just a dream*, thinks the girl. *He's never been anything but a dream.* The girl turns to leave, but then looks back at the piles of books. She wants to say something, explain something to these piles of books that have the power to look like the boy. 'I need to get some concrete screws,' she tells them. She closes the door.

It's so quiet with the boy gone. Some days, the girl likes this. She comes down to the kitchen and plugs in the kettle. She listens to it hum, then seethe, as the water comes to a boil. Other days, all she can hear is the sound of her own heart coming to a stop, then firing up again, over and over.

'I feel like there is an infinite assortment of words sitting in places all over the house,' said the boy. The girl looked up from her salad. 'That's the way I feel, too,' she said. She looked back at her plate, lifted a forkful of lettuce to her mouth. She chewed for a while. They were dining at the coffee table in the living room by the light of the floor lamp with the trilight bulb. They had the bulb on the lowest intensity, which the boy liked to think was reminiscent of candlelight.

'We're just a story in the boy's head,' the girl tells the cat as she plops some food into its bowl. *Or he's a story in my head*, she thinks. *He hasn't really disappeared. He isn't really gone, because he was never really here.* 'But what about the journals?' she asks the cat as she sets its bowl on the floor. The cat eats. The girl goes downstairs to check on the journals. She feels anxious, like the journals might not be there, like they might have disappeared. Like when a time traveller steps on a prehistoric insect and everything that insect spawned on down through eternity disappears. Or maybe the boy came back to spirit the journals away in the middle of the night while the girl was upstairs asleep in bed. The girl has been feeling afraid that if she doesn't keep track of the journals, if she doesn't keep them safe, one day she'll find them gone. She can hear the cat's paws padding down the stairs as it follows her. 'No one has disappeared,' she says to the cat when it appears like some fluffy apparition in the doorway. 'It's just another one of the boy's stories.' The journals are still there on the floor in the basement where the boy left them. The girl is surprised when she realizes that she almost wished they'd been gone this time.

Dick followed an angel into the afterlife. The angel dressed Dick in a white robe and laid him out on a bed of clouds. She took care of Dick and tended to his needs. But in the end it seemed that Dick had no real needs, so the angel sent him back to his living room. Dick sat on the couch watching TV, waiting for the day when the angel would invite him back to the afterlife.

It was night. The boy and the girl were in a bus station, one of those old stations, poorly lit, with high ceilings and concrete benches along the walls. One wall was all windows. The entire station was cold. The girl had just come back from a summer job up north and was on her way to visit a friend in Sarnia. The boy was getting ready to go back to university. They could see dirty rainwater flying up off the tires of buses going by outside. They were sitting on one of the concrete benches that ran along the back wall of the station. An announcement came on the public address system. 'That's my bus,' said the girl. The boy looked at her. They stood up. The boy hugged the girl. The girl hugged him back. She picked up her bag and went out of the station. The boy stayed where he was, standing by the bench, until he saw the girl's bus go by the window and he was all alone again.

The grinder whines. Then it stops. The girl pulls out the hopper, scoops out coffee, puts it in the filter. She stares at it. She's put in too much. She needs only enough for one.

The girl sits among the piles of journals in the basement, reading at random, silence echoing in her head, filling the emptiness left from her trying to resurrect the boy. She feels him limp toward her like an injured animal at the side of the road, barely alive, unable to make a sound. She can't keep doing this. She can't keep picking up pieces of the boy like this, then setting them down as though nothing has changed. She needs to make something happen. Clean up this mess, get things organized. Or just throw everything out. She scoops up a pile of the journals and carries them upstairs. She stands in the middle of the kitchen, still unsure. Finally, she sets them down on the kitchen table. She goes over to the counter by the sink, intending to make a cup of coffee, but then she turns back to look at the journals.

She's been keeping them where she found them, in the boy's little hiding places around the house, and in the tottering piles in the basement. But why not just keep them on the table so that they're here for her to read whenever the mood strikes? At the very least, she'll be closer to the coffee machine. She goes downstairs and brings up another pile. She feels better, setting it next to the others. She can make a checklist. Keep track of what she's read. Keep things moving forward. She goes downstairs to get more journals. When she's got them all up from the basement, she steps back to look at them. They cover most of the table. She feels like she's finally taken some real steps – toward what, though? For a moment, she feels a sense of panic, like she's just said something terrible to the boy and it's too late to take it back. She grabs one of the piles and rushes downstairs. She stands in the doorway to the rec room, trying to resurrect the castle of books in her mind. The room looks so empty. The carpet is like a scar.

The voice of Dick's phone whispered something and Dick got up out of bed. A cloud of sound came in through the open window, along with some spring air that touched Dick on places he liked to be touched. Dick put on a shirt and went over to the window. A group of girls was standing outside on the sidewalk. They looked like they were in high school and sounded like they were high. They giggled together in the cool spring air and chattered away in a language Dick couldn't understand. He went back and sat down on the bed, his bare feet on the orange throw rug he'd put there to keep his feet warm. The voices of the high school girls grew far off. They drifted like thin bits of silky thread pulled upward into a windy sky, and then they disappeared and Dick was alone again in the silence.

'It felt like flight,' says the woman. She's maybe twenty, a university student who, according to the text under the video, is finding it very hard to get back into her studies now that she's returned. 'It was like running alone in the dark through a snowstorm,' she says. 'I thought of things I might do. Or … ' she's stumbling over her words ' … it was like I'd been doing something, and now it came to light that I'd been doing it all along.' She narrows her eyes. 'There was a moment when I realized I was doing something, and that was the end of me doing it. So there was an end.' Her eyes widen and she raises a hand. 'I could see the end. Which means there must be a now, right?' She looks at the camera, her eyes bright with ferocious light. The interviewer mumbles something and the student lets out a sharp laugh. 'You think?' she asks. 'But that doesn't seem likely,' she says, half to herself. 'I mean, it would probably be easier.' She looks pensive. 'I don't seem to be learning anything here anymore, anyway. I mean, it wasn't like I learned anything while I was gone. It was like there was nothing to learn there. Or like everything I needed to know I already knew.' The girl thinks about rewinding it to find out what the interviewer asked to prompt this line of thought from the student, but she feels like this would be conceding something to the interviewer, and she decides she's not going to do that.

When the girl walks into the room and sees the cat sitting like a buddha in the middle of the floor, she pushes her hair away from her face and scoops the creature up into her arms, as though gathering up a doll that was handmade by a dearly beloved, long-dead aunt.

The girl woke. The boy was sitting up beside her in the bed, the side of his face lit by the nightlight they had plugged into the outlet in the corner of the room. The girl stayed on her side, head sinking into her pillow, covers up to her chin. She shifted, pulling in her knees. 'I had a dream that we were at the beach and the waves were getting bigger and bigger,' she said quietly, 'until, finally, one washed right up into the cottage.' She couldn't tell if the boy was even listening to her. 'I was sitting on the toilet and the water came in under the door, and I knew I was in trouble.' The girl pulled a pillow tight to her stomach. 'There was a woman in the bathroom with me,' she went on. 'I hadn't known she was there in the dream until she said: "I saw that one coming." She was sitting behind me on the toilet tank.' The girl peeked over at the boy. He seemed to be in some sort of a trance, staring straight ahead, maybe not even aware that the girl was there. 'The woman in the dream was young. Thin. Wearing a halter top and shorts, her brown hair bobbed around her ears. Her voice filled the dream, becoming a kind of hum that stayed with me long after I had woken up and gone down to the kitchen to make coffee.' She stopped. 'You made coffee?' the boy asked. He looked down at the girl. 'Yes,' said the girl. 'A couple hours ago, but I didn't drink it.' 'How much coffee did you make?' asked the boy. 'Just a cup,' said the girl, 'but we can split it.' 'Okay,' said the boy. 'It's probably not a good idea to have a whole cup anyway. Not at this hour.' 'No, probably not,' said the girl. She got their housecoats off the hook on the back of the door and handed one to the boy. They put on the housecoats and made their way down to the kitchen.

Late in the night, the girl wakes up and remembers crowds she's had to navigate, puddles she's had to go around, cracks in the sidewalk. She sees all the meaningless little things that happened to her throughout the day. They are lying close by her in the dark, these meaningless moments, waiting for her to find them again, as though reliving them here in bed in the middle of the night might give them sudden meaning.

The icy wind sweeps down from the north, pushing the girl's hair past her face, rushing to get to wherever it is they are going before the girl can get there. She turns and turns and turns again, spinning like a top that wants to be a helicopter.

The boy was beside the girl, holding her hand. Neither of them talked. The residential street they were on ended and they crossed into a commercial area. The roads were busier here. Noisier. Buses and trucks of all sizes wove in and out among cars that caterwauled around corners and lurched away from stoplights. The sidewalks were filled with people on their way to work. They went south on Grace and arrived at Dundas. The girl had thought they were going to hit Queen Street next. She'd forgotten about Dundas.

FEBRUARY

The cat disappears on Valentine's Day. The girl checks the internet. There's nothing she can find about animals disappearing. *Surely there'd be something on the internet if people's cats started disappearing,* she thinks. *People love their cats more than they love their people.* Later in the day, when the girl is sitting in the living room wrapped in a blanket, paging through a magazine, the cat crawls out from underneath the couch. The girl laughs, sets her magazine down on the coffee table, and picks up the cat. When she puts it down a long while later, she has fur stuck to her face where it's wet with her tears.

When the girl gets home, she goes to the window. God is standing in the snowy street in front of the house. *What's she doing out there?* the girl wonders. She's afraid God might want to move into the garage again. *I'll just tell her no, she can't live in our garage anymore.* She goes down to the front door and looks through the peephole. *God looks so tiny,* the girl thinks, laughing at herself for being so afraid. For a long time, she just stares through the peephole. *I can't just leave her out there,* she thinks in the end. She goes out and stands beside God. 'I've been walking for hours, just thinking,' says God. 'Come inside,' says the girl. 'You don't even have a coat on. It's cold. What are you doing out here without a coat on? You need to dress for the weather.' When they get inside, God takes off her shoes and goes into the living room. She sits in the easy chair. The girl sits on the couch across from her. After a time, the girl gets up to make coffee. She has some muffins, too, from Costco. They are big muffins. The girl gets one out for God. She puts it on a plate. Gives God a napkin. 'It's nice and warm in here,' God says, smiling at the girl.

The boy was standing in the middle of the kitchen, holding his journal. The girl was at the counter, her hands in the sink. 'Dick pushed hard on the pedals of his bicycle,' the boy said. He didn't seem to be reading, just spilling, like an overflowing toilet. He was looking at the back of the girl like he could see something there, like maybe Dick riding his bike across the back of her PJ top. 'Dick's bicycle was red.' His words came slowly. 'With silver trim.' He looked down at the floor. 'Dick could hear another bicycle coming up the road behind him.' He paused. He didn't even have the journal open now. He'd closed it, keeping one hand on top, like he was swearing on a Bible. The girl stopped washing the bowl she was holding and turned around to look at the boy. She thought she could hear the other bike coming up the road behind her. 'Dick could hear tires crunching gravel,' the boy continued. The girl put a fingernail between her front teeth. 'Dick turned. *Fuck*, he said to himself. He couldn't yet see who it was. He didn't want to see who it was. He tried to pedal harder, but his trick knee was acting up. It was 8:00 a.m. and the sun was hot already.'

The girl is wide awake, lying on her back. She sits up, drops her legs over the edge of the bed. It's too early to be up. She thinks about crawling back under the covers. She knows she won't be able to go back to sleep. She gets up off the bed, goes to the window, opens the curtains. The sky is red. There's a light dusting of snow on the ground. The smell of the cold seeps through the bedroom wall, mixing with the chemical aroma of heat from the air duct at her feet. The girl knows what to do. She goes everywhere around the house, getting all the journals she knows of, plus a few she stumbles across that she's never seen before, and piles them onto the kitchen table with the ones she's brought up from the basement.

God was sitting in a big leather armchair in the garage. Dick was lying on a blow-up mattress set atop the freezer. 'You need to be more honest with yourself, Dick,' God said. 'You need to tell people what you're really thinking.' Dick had his eyes closed. He was picturing God as Sigmund Freud stroking his greying beard, notepad open in his lap. When Dick opened his eyes, he saw that God had turned himself into a woman, and she was naked. He thought he could smell what was happening between her legs.

'I was thinking of Sigmund Freud,' said the boy. The girl laughed. The boy grinned and shook his head. 'Dumb, right?' 'No, no,' said the girl, 'I was actually thinking maybe it was Sigmund Freud you were thinking of.' The boy pulled his head back. 'You were not,' he said. The girl laughed and got up from where they were sitting together on the couch. She grabbed the boy's hand and pulled at him to get up.

Kids in mittens tug at their mothers' hands. Men in dress shoes disappear into blowing snow. Inside the front entrance to the store, the girl stamps her boots. She pulls off her hat and gives it a shake. She tries to brush the snow off her shoulders. She grabs a buggy, shows the lady at the door her membership card, and goes into the store. When she gets to the area with the clothing, she picks up a men's dress shirt. She holds it by the hanger, dangling it in front of her face, then turns it around to look at the back. She pulls down the collar. 'A hundred per cent cotton,' she whispers. She looks up to see if anyone is watching. No one seems remotely interested. She looks back at the shirt, folds it twice, and sets it in the cart. *This is stupid*, she thinks as she turns into the dairy aisle. *Even if the boy does come back, the last thing he needs is another shirt.*

In the middle of February, the air warmed and all the snow melted, but now it's back. The girl is still finding journals stashed in odd places around the house. Standing in the kitchen, close to the window, looking out at the street, she's holding one that she found at the back of the cupboard with the cleaning supplies. She looks down at it, feeling something that stands on the border between joy and pain. She has no desire to open the journal. She is almost afraid to open it. She's afraid this might be the last one. She likes coming across new journals. She doesn't want this to stop. She wants to wander around the house like this forever, stumbling across pieces of the boy at her leisure, discovering these journals and then … what? She's been tossing them onto the kitchen table, intending to read them at some point. But she doesn't think the idea of reading them is what keeps her from throwing them all out. It's more like having the warmth of the boy beside her in bed, but without him wanting to paw at her all the time. It's as though she likes the idea of the boy between the journal's covers more than she likes what she actually finds there.

Dick is sitting in the back seat of the car playing with one of his dolls. His mother is driving. She stops at a red light and looks up at Dick, the way he's framed in the mirror, the way the light coming in the back window illuminates the edges of his hair. She feels like a taxi driver with a beautiful young man in the back. 'Where to, sir?' she says. Dick goes on dressing his dolly. He doesn't look up when he speaks to his mother. 'We'd like to go home now,' he says, buttoning up his dolly's blouse.

The girl was outside looking into the living room. The boy was sitting on the couch in his gotchies. The girl seemed to be saying something, but the boy couldn't hear her. He could see her mouth moving, as though she was forming words, but he couldn't be sure that she wasn't just opening and closing her mouth like a fish in a fish tank. He could hear the kitchen timer ticking. He kept looking at the girl where she stood on the other side of the glass, her bottom lip hanging lower on one side than on the other. Her lips looked chapped, but at the same time wet. She was licking them, and sucking on them, pulling her lower lip into her mouth and kneading it with her teeth. Her eyes seemed uneven. It hurt the boy to look at the girl's face this way. He closed his eyes and tried to remember her face in his mind. When he opened his eyes again, he saw that the girl's face was quite different from how he'd imagined it when he'd had his eyes closed. He closed his eyes again. A long time later, he opened them and the girl was gone. Dark clouds covered the sky.

In the middle of the night, the girl wakes up thinking about all the journals down on the kitchen table. She feels around in the dark for the cat and locates it with her feet. She pushes the covers down to her waist, then slides her legs out and hangs them over the edge of the bed. She reaches for the lamp on her bedside table. The cat lifts its head when the light comes on, blinks at the girl, yawns widely, then puts its paw over its eyes and goes back to sleep. The girl goes downstairs to make coffee. While it's brewing, she gets out a roll of masking tape and a sharpie. She starts to number the journals. By the time she's numbered the final journal '143,' it's growing light outside. The girl pours a third cup of coffee and sits down at the table with journal number one. She opens it to page one. She takes a sip of coffee. The cat comes in and stands by its food dish. It looks at the girl silently for a moment and, when the girl doesn't get up, starts yowling. The girl gets the tin of food from the fridge and scoops some into the bowl. She stands above the cat, listening to the sound of it licking the food. The smell is disgusting but somehow reassuring. The girl goes back to the table, takes a final sip of coffee, closes journal number one, and goes back up to bed.

It's early morning when Dick gets out of bed and goes to the window. He looks out at the parking lot below. There's snow on the cars. It's too late in the year for snow, Dick thinks. But there it is. A woman is brushing snow off her blue car. She's wearing a very short skirt and an even shorter coat. She must be cold, Dick thinks. He can see her breath. She swishes the brush across the front windshield a few times, then gets in the car, turns on the wipers, and drives away. Exhaust hangs in the air where the car has been.

God gets out of a white car and stands under a street light in the falling snow. The girl is up the street a ways, hoping God doesn't see her. She thinks about the boy. *He'd go over and talk to God,* she thinks. *He'd invite God to go for coffee.* The boy is too nice, the girl decides. Or he tries too hard to be nice. *I try to be nice,* thinks the girl. *It's not bad to be nice.* The boy used to set the cat food dish on a little stand he'd ordered online so that the cat wouldn't have to strain its neck. The stand was always filthy. The boy never cleaned it. There were bits of hardened cat food stuck to it, no doubt mixed with cat drool and god knows what else. The girl looks back up the street to see what God is doing, but she's gone. When the girl gets home, she picks up the cat food stand, intending to clean it, but then she opens the cupboard under the sink and tosses the filthy thing into the garbage.

The girl touched the boy's back. She moved her hand up to his neck. The boy made a sound. He tried to see the girl's face through the darkness. The girl stared into space, as though the boy wasn't there, as though the boy was too far beyond where she was for him to ever fit into the space she inhabited. The boy was too far away to be anything but a blurry shape. The girl giggled. 'What?' said the boy. He pulled his head back, tried again to look at the girl's face.

'I was ten when I disappeared,' says the old man. *That can't be right*, thinks the girl. She taps at the laptop to make the video rewind. The old man says it again. 'I was ten.' He stabs himself in the chest with his finger. His eyes go wide. 'Now look at me,' he says. The girl looks at him. He must be at least eighty. *Maybe the boy won't come back till he's eighty*, she thinks. *I could be dead by then*. She feels strangely relieved, like when she and the boy booked a vacation a year in advance and she started to worry right away, but then realized she didn't have to worry about it yet. But then the time passed so quickly, and suddenly she did have to worry about it. *I can't wait around any longer*, she realizes. 'It was like being stuck in a place I couldn't get out of,' the old guy says, but the girl isn't really listening. She wants to get up, get on with things, stop watching these videos. 'But I didn't want to get out of it,' says the old man. 'I didn't want to stay either. I didn't want anything. I felt like I'd never want anything again. I simply didn't want.' The girl realizes that she doesn't want anything either. She doesn't want the boy to come back. She doesn't want him to stay away. But she does want … something. She just doesn't know what. The old geezer looks thoughtful. 'And it didn't feel like any time was passing,' he says. 'It was like I was gone and then back in an instant.' It's hard to tell what the old guy might be feeling. His eyes are white, covered over with cataracts. He could be grinning. Or grimacing. *He looks like a monster*, the girl thinks. 'But when I was there,' he says, 'wherever it was I was, there was no sense of time passing.' He stutters to a stop. There's an old woman in a rocking chair behind him, rocking back and forth, smiling and nodding at what the old boy is saying. She looks even older than her husband. She looks like she's part of the rocking chair, like she's tied down to it with cobwebs and she couldn't get out of it if she tried. The interviewer calls out: 'What did you think when your husband disappeared, ma'am?' It's the first time the girl can understand clearly what the interviewer is saying. *Probably the old girl is deaf*, thinks the girl, *so the interviewer has to yell.* The interviewer's voice sounds vaguely feminine. After the interviewer shouts his question, the old girl says nothing for a time, just goes on smiling and rocking. When she finally speaks, it's impossible to tell what she's saying. She's too far away from the microphone, which is on the lapel of the old man's bathrobe. The camera moves, jerking around till it's pointing at the old man's lap. There's a loud raspy noise, then the camera moves again, toward the old lady. A hand appears in front of the camera and clips the lapel mic to the old lady's bathrobe. The camera moves back. *Doesn't this guy know how to edit a video?* the girl thinks. 'Could you repeat what you just said, ma'am,' the interviewer says. 'I said,' the old woman shouts, 'that I didn't even know him when he disappeared.' She looks at the camera like the guy behind it is an idiot. 'He was ten,' she says, shouting even louder. *These two old farts must have dementia,* the girl thinks. *The old guy probably never disappeared anywhere but into his own disease-ridden mind.*

God stood out in the roadway stopping the neighbours' cars. The girl watched her through the front window. She called to the boy, who was in the bathroom washing his face. 'What?' the boy called. He towelled his face and went out to see what the girl wanted. When he saw what was going on outside, he opened the window. 'Hey,' he called. God turned. 'What are you doing?' God held her hand above her eyes to block out the sun. 'I need to get to the mall,' she said. The boy swore. 'I can drive you,' he called. 'You need to stop bothering the neighbours.' 'They don't mind,' said God, 'but if you have time to drive me, that would be great.' She trotted up the driveway, closer to the window. 'Could you maybe lend me some money as well?' she asked, keeping her voice low.

In a way, having the boy's journals is as good as having the boy, but without having to deal with the actual boy. The girl can sit and peruse them at her leisure. She can wander, as though each of the journals is a room full of stuff the boy has left lying around. The way he used to leave his clothes on the bedroom floor, and his books and papers on the coffee table in the living room, and his towel on the bathroom counter, and the newly cleaned laundry unfolded in a heap on top of the dryer. Sitting in the morning sun in the kitchen with these journals, having this mess of words to confront, makes the girl feel like the boy is still there, even though he's not still there. Like she can talk to him, tell him the truth, say, 'Quit being such a doofus,' but without having to see his face after she has hurt his feelings.

Dick walks toward the moon. He's lost in a big city he's never been in, trying to find a woman he has never met. He's been wandering for hours when he thinks he spots her way up ahead on a corner under a street light. She looks like an actor standing on a stage looking melancholy under a single spot. Dick is far up in the theatre's nosebleeds, swooning as he watches her perform. But it isn't a street light that is spotlighting the woman, Dick suddenly sees, nor is it a spotlight. It's the moon, and it's moving away. Dick tries to follow, but it disappears behind a building, and by the time Dick gets around to the other side, the moon is gone, along with the woman he has never met.

Now that the boy is gone, the girl can take his words and bring him back. Or send him away. She can piece the boy together, or tear him apart. It won't matter. She can't hurt him. She can just let him go. Or she can gather him up the way she used to when they came home and crawled into each other's arms at the end of their long day apart. One or the other. *It's time to decide,* the girl decides. She tips the journal she's presently reading toward the cat. 'Look at this,' she says. 'No sign of Dick at all.' She skims ahead, running her fingers across the page like feeling for Braille. She puts her hand on the cat's head when she sees Dick's name appear again. But Dick, once again, does nothing. Goes nowhere.

Dick passes someone on the street. Then he passes someone else. Each person he passes is full of secrets. Secrets fall around like rain splashing into puddles. Or dandelion seeds floating on the wind. Dick looks back over his shoulder through the misty rain. He thinks he sees a woman far off in the distance, receding into the past, moving away from him, twirling her bright orange umbrella and skipping through puddles in her yellow rubber boots.

'We need to get that freezer out of the garage,' said the girl. The boy didn't answer right away. When he did, he seemed to be choosing his words carefully. 'I think,' he said, 'that God might be sleeping on it.' 'What?' said the girl. 'You mean she's down there sleeping on the new freezer?' 'Well, she's not sleeping on it at this very moment,' said the boy. 'Although she might be,' he added, looking at his watch. 'She might be taking a nap.' The boy looked at the girl's face, then hurried to finish what he was saying. 'I mean, I think she's using it for a bed. Not necessarily right now. But, you know, just generally.' 'Just generally!' exclaimed the girl. She walked around the kitchen a little, as though she was going to do some cleaning up, or maybe explode, but then she stopped by the sink and said very slowly, enunciating each word: 'God cannot sleep on our new freezer. Tell that cunt to stay off our new freezer.' The boy stepped back. 'Don't say that,' he said. The girl scowled, then looked amused, like she'd just thought of something funny. 'Don't say what?' she said, taunting the boy. 'That God can't sleep on our freezer?' she asked. 'You know what I mean,' said the boy, 'don't say that word.' 'What word?' said the girl, almost smiling. 'Don't say it,' said the boy. 'Tell me what word,' said the girl, 'and I promise not to say it.' 'No,' said the boy. 'Say it,' said the girl. 'No,' said the boy. The girl laughed and shook her head. 'Tell God she has to find another place to sleep,' she said, and went out of the kitchen. The boy looked down. The sun shining in the window made a path across the kitchen floor that ended partway up the boy's ankle. When he wiggled his toes, the bones on the top of his foot did a little dance beneath the skin.

SPRING

The boy disappeared into his journals long before he ever actually disappeared. *He disappeared into Dick*, thinks the girl. She butters a piece of toast and lifts it to her mouth, but then stops and sets it back onto the plate without taking a bite. She laughs. *He's gone to Dickville*, she thinks. She goes upstairs, gets the boy's laptop, opens Google Maps. She types 'Dickville' into the search box. It's in West Wyoming. That's where the boy is, she decides. West Wyoming. She stares down at her toast. If she wants to find the boy, she just has to go to West Wyoming. She clicks the 'Directions' button. She can be there in six hours and eleven minutes. She puts her hands on the table and pushes herself up. She stands above the table, looking down at her toast.

The girl begins again to wonder if maybe *she* isn't the one who has disappeared. Maybe she's in some alternate universe, like she's read about on the internet, and the boy is in the same place he always was, the place where she thinks she is, and he's back where they were, where she thought she was all along, alone without the boy. *He's back there all alone without me now*, she thinks. This makes her sad, but then she realizes her sadness is not for the boy, but for herself, and this makes her angry. She stares out the window at nothing. *Serves you right, you fucker*, she says in her mind, although it's not clear to her whether she's talking to herself or the boy.

'One time, when we were first going out, I fell asleep on your lawn,' said the boy. The girl looked surprised. 'It was late at night,' said the boy. 'You weren't with me. You'd already gone in.' The girl could feel the boy inside her. *This is the place I thought I wanted to be,* she was thinking. *But it's like a trap, and there's no escape.* 'I could feel your hands on me,' said the boy. 'You were in your house. And I was out on the front lawn.' *I am the boy's house,* thought the girl. *He's merely seeking shelter.* 'There are no rules,' whispered the boy. 'I understand this.' He was back on the girl's front lawn, lying in the damp grass by himself, smelling the night air and watching the moon move slowly through the branches of the trees that towered above him. And he knew it was okay to live in a world without rules. He sank. *This is a new world,* he said to himself before he fell asleep.

The girl watches her hands move of their own accord, like tissue freed of bones. They reach across the table and take hold of a journal. She's given up trying to read them all, or even read them in any sort of order. Or even read them, really. She opens the journal to a page in the middle and feels her finger run along the page. She watches it move across the scrawling sea of words that the boy has dumped overboard. Her fingers float above the words, skimming the boy's meaning like a water skier watching for the right moment to let go and sink slowly down into the dark water.

Dick tipped his head up and looked down over his body, past his feet. There were sandpipers playing in the foamy water lapping at the shore. He let his head fall back. He went to sleep. The warmth of the sun on his face was the hands of his mother caressing his cheeks.

'There were times when I did think about trying to get away from the boy,' the girl tells the cat, which is attacking its food like it hasn't eaten in days. The girl tries to remember if she fed it last night. 'Sometimes he drove me crazy,' she says. She puts her hand on the cat's back. 'Slow down,' she says, 'or you'll make yourself sick.' The cat feels so warm. 'The boy was like that,' says the girl. 'He was like a furnace. It was good in the winter at night. But in the summer, I just wanted to push him out of the bed.' The cat gobbles up the last of its food, gives the dish a thorough licking, and sits down to wash its face. The girl goes around to the living room and picks up the journal she was reading before she went to bed last night. After a time, the cat arrives and pushes its head against her leg. The girl sets the journal down on the coffee table. She bends to stroke the cat. The cat falls on its side on the rug. Offers the girl its belly. The girl gets down on her knees. She kneads the cat's belly. The cat rolls its head back. The girl settles onto the rug beside the cat and lays her head on its belly. She feels the hard roar of the cat's purr penetrate her ear.

There is a new god in the town, so the girl goes to visit. The new god lives at 2115 Sunnydale Boulevard, not far from where the girl's friend Kitty lived back when they were in high school. It's a lovely spring day, so the girl walks. She knocks on the door. For a long time, she waits, looking around at the new god's garden. She likes the way the new god has arranged her marigolds. She knocks again, then stands back from the door and peers around at the front window. She can see the curtains moving. *I guess that's the new god,* she tells herself. She steps forward and knocks more forcefully. She looks around for a doorbell.

What if I were to rip all the words out of all the boy's journals, thinks the girl, closing the journal she's been reading and getting up off the bed. *I could scatter them around the room, like flower petals. Each word would become a shape, but nothing else. I could gather them together and organize them by the shapes they make.* She drifts around the house, carrying the journals in her hands, like she's dancing at a wedding, trying to decide if this would be a good time to throw some confetti. She decides to start in the basement. On her way down, she stops off in the kitchen and grabs as many of the journals as she can carry. In the basement, she drops the journals onto the ugly orange rug. She steps back and looks at the pile. It looks nice. Almost as nice as the way the boy had them piled before he disappeared. *Nicer, really*, thinks the girl. She tries to decide which one to start with. *Does it even matter?* she wonders. It's like trying to decide whether to use a frozen loaf of bread to make a sandwich or to play a game of football.

Out the kitchen window, the girl watched the boy walking along the sidewalk in front of the house. He walked past the house, then continued on for a half a block, before turning around and walking past the house again in the other direction. He went back and forth like this, back and forth, back and forth. The way the boy was walking was the strangest thing the girl had ever seen. He walked with his head down, hunched over. His torso seemed to float on an unwavering axis, legs pumping beneath him like train wheels hitched to invisible bars that joined him at the knees. Watching the boy walk back and forth like that was making the girl feel mildly sick, vaguely hungry. The boy was wearing a black knit cap. It looked like he was trying to grow a beard. The beard looked not like whiskers but like light-coloured dirt rubbed onto his cheeks, as if he'd fallen face-first into the garden and couldn't be bothered to tidy himself up.

'It felt like I was safe,' says a woman in what looks like a jester's cap. *Why is she wearing that hat?* thinks the girl. The woman's nose is pierced and she's got earrings that dangle almost to her shoulders. Her braids, which hang down past her shoulders, are green. Her midriff is bare and her belly button is pierced. 'It was like whatever was going on,' says the woman, ' – and I had no idea what was going on – I was going to survive this whole adventure, because that's what this was, another life adventure. You have to believe that whatever comes your way, it's part of your adventure, don't you think?' She looks at the camera. The interviewer says something that the girl can't decipher, and then the video cuts to a thirty-second mid-stream advertisement with no 'Skip Ad' option. 'Has someone you love disappeared?' a voice asks. The voice sounds suspiciously like the interviewer, only much clearer. As the narration begins, the screen is black, but gradually a swirl of pastel colours grows from the centre, finally resolving into a human being standing in a field of wild-flowers. *Is that the interviewer?* the girl wonders. *He looks so young.* It's a short ad. 'I can help you find your loved ones,' the guy says as the ad winds down. A URL appears at the bottom of the screen, and then it cuts back to the interview. 'I thought maybe I was dead,' says the woman in the jester's cap. 'It felt a bit like being dead. I mean, I don't know what it feels like to be dead, obviously.' She shrugs, laughs, and the bobbles on her hat jiggle. 'But it felt like a release, sort of, the way maybe death could feel, you know?' The jester grins. The interviewer says some-thing, and the girl tries to listen to see if it's the same voice as the ad. 'It wasn't like I saw my life flash before my eyes or anything,' says the jester. 'More like I was telling my own story, a story that was over, so it could be told. But I didn't care that it was over. I was glad it was over.' She looks a bit startled, like she's just figured this out. Her teeth are crooked but very white. 'You know,' she says, 'I really do believe I was glad it was over. It's only now that I'm back that I've started to question these emotions. Or not really emotions. More like a vacancy. A pleasant emptiness. Like a lack of pain. Like, you know, you wake up one morning and realize that the headache you've had for three days is gone. You don't even notice at first. You get up out of bed, you put on your slippers, or whatever it is you do when you first get out of bed, and you're going about your business, when suddenly you realize that the pain is gone.' The jester smiles. Her skin looks very healthy. 'Only it was more like there was never any pain, I just thought there was pain, and now I was suddenly aware of the fact that there'd never been any pain.' The interviewer speaks and a sad smile lights the jester's eyes. 'No,' she says, 'the pain is back. Like it was never gone. Like I just wasn't aware of it while I was … where I was.' The jester smiles one last time and the screen goes blank. The girl clicks the Replay button. She wants to see that hat again. And that beguiling smile.

The girl comes in from the cold. She goes to the front hall closet and searches through the coats, looking for an empty hanger. There aren't any. She pulls out a hanger with a coat already on it, takes off the coat she is wearing and drapes it over the coat that was already on the hanger. She shoves the two coats into the mess of coats already stuffed in there. *I should take the boy's coats out of here and put them somewhere else*, thinks the girl. *It's not like he's using them.* She stares at the coats. *I don't know where I'd put them, though.* She breathes out. *I should just get rid of them*, she tells herself. *Give them to the Goodwill.* She closes the closet and goes into the kitchen to feed the cat.

Something is nagging at the girl when she wakes up at 5:00 a.m., but she can't figure out what it is. Is it something she dreamed? No, it was something in the journal she was reading last night before she went to bed. She sits up and rubs her face. It's hot in the bedroom. She goes downstairs and turns up the air conditioning. Then she goes to the kitchen table. She tries to figure out which journal she was reading last night, but she can't be sure. She takes one off the top of the pile and opens it. She thumbs through the pages, trying to find the correct passage. This doesn't seem to be the journal she wants. She goes to set it back down onto the table, but thinks better of it and simply drops it on the floor. She picks up another one. After paging through four journals this way, she gives up and just stands there staring at the pile. Then she reaches both arms across the table and heaves all the journals onto the floor. She laughs a laugh that threatens to go out of control, then plunks down onto the floor amid the journals. She picks one up at random and opens it.

A woman Dick had never seen was standing at the counter in her nightie, her back to Dick, spreading butter on a piece of toast. She pushed her hair away from her face with her arm. Then she stayed very still, looking down at her toast. She had the knife raised up in the air with a gob of butter on it, but she didn't lower it to the toast. 'God said I should try to be more honest with people,' said Dick. The woman lowered the knife and scraped it across the toast slowly. Then she picked up her plate and took it to the table, where she sat down and ate her toast while Dick stood motionless, watching.

The girl takes the rest of the boy's journals that have been sitting on the kitchen floor for days and carts them down to the basement. She heaps them with the others on the ugly rug. She closes her eyes and snatches one from the top of the pile. She opens it, intent on tearing it to pieces, but before she can do it, she finds herself reading about Dick again.

Dick was up the street and around the corner from the shoe store in the middle of town. He knew his mother was somewhere – she couldn't have just disappeared – but he couldn't seem to find her. Last he saw her, she was walking past the post office. Dick had come uptown to buy some shoes at the old shoe store. He'd swung around when he heard the sound of footsteps, but it was just some woman in high heels and a short skirt pushing a blue baby carriage.

The girl gets in her car, puts on her sunglasses, adjusts the car's mirrors, tilts the wheel down, turns the ignition key. The engine fires. When she gets out to the main street, she parks, gets out. Noises rise around her. A lady in heels clicks by along the sidewalk. 'Will the sun ever return?' asks a man. The girl looks up at the sky. The sun is not really gone, she wants to tell the man. It *will* come back.

'I couldn't remember where anyone was,' says a guy in sandals, shorts, and an untucked Hawaiian shirt. He's sitting under what looks to the girl like a coconut tree. 'Then I remembered: no one was.' He speaks slowly, calmly, as though paddling about aimlessly in a warm sea full of words. 'And then,' he says, raising a finger – but he stops to look at his finger. He twists it in the air, tipping his head to see it at different angles, like it's some kind of glittery object floating in front of his face. The interviewer says something and the guy looks up at the camera. He smiles languidly. 'I remembered,' he says, 'that the who who I was couldn't actually remember the why of who no one is.' His face goes goofy. The girl doesn't want to look at him anymore, but she goes on looking. She can't seem to stop herself. 'And it didn't really matter,' the guy says, 'why no one was,' he rubs the peach fuzz on his cheek, 'or how the who I was came to remember the why of who I wasn't, or the who of who I thought I could never be.' *What the fuck*, thinks the girl. 'And then I remembered that the why of why no one was wasn't the matter, because there was no matter.' The guy grins and shakes his head, sits back against the tree. Nothing happens for a long moment. The guy looks like he might be asleep. The interviewer says something and the guy sits up and blinks. Then the camera goes off.

The girl believes that she might be coming to know things about the boy that even the boy doesn't know. By reading his words, by piecing him together one word at a time, she might finally be coming to know things about him. But she also knows that what she knows about the boy that he doesn't know isn't something she could know enough to show him. It isn't something she might carry toward the boy and bring back to him, like a stone tablet or a sheaf of papyrus. Or a notebook. It's more like the sort of thing she comes to know about the boy when she touches him with the tip of her tongue on the tip of his earlobe.

The girl closes the journal in her lap. Part of her wants to go on reading, but it's like being trapped in the small space that separates Dick from the boy, like the two of them are hemming her in, standing on either side of her, squeezing, making it impossible to move. She takes a deep breath. Holds it. But then she can't help resuming the shallow rapid breathing that is making her light-headed to the point where she thinks she might pass out. Her hands feel numb and her mouth is dry. She thinks she might throw up. She wants to despise Dick. But hating Dick feels too close to hating the boy, and she isn't ready for that.

The girl pulls open the sandwich she's been eating and looks inside. 'What's in this thing?' she whispers. As she breathes out, it feels like this is going to be her last breath. It's a good feeling; a feeling of relief.

When she finds the boy's old sandals on the floor at the back of the linen closet, the girl doesn't know what to think. The boy used to come to her with old stuff – shoes, socks, underwear he wasn't wearing anymore – and ask her if he should give them to the Goodwill. What did he think? That people wanted his used underwear? The girl tries to summon the boy in her mind, hear his voice, see his face. She holds up the sandals, as though that might help her channel him. They look like pretty good shoes. But the girl would never buy somebody else's used shoes. You could get some kind of disease. She goes down to the kitchen and gets out a plastic bag. She puts the shoes in the bag, then takes the bag down to the basement and puts it with the heap of journals. *The boy's not coming back*, she thinks. And even if he does, she decides, he's probably going to be like one of these nut jobs she keeps seeing in YouTube interviews.

In everything the girl finds on the internet, in all the interviews with people who have returned, no one seems to be able to explain what happened to them while they were gone. They are gone, and then they are back. Nothing happens to them in between. But it seems, in every case, as if something has happened to them. Something is changing these people, even though they swear, every one of them, that nothing has changed. Something is changing in the world, they seem to be saying, but whatever it is that is changing, has always already been changing, and the place where these people are disappearing to seems to be a place where it's possible to see this change in the world that no one in the world can really see because being in the world means being the change. It all seems scary to the girl, like a movie where they constantly jiggle the camera. These people who have disappeared and come back seem to want to disappear again, and this terrifies the girl.

The girl was naked at the bathroom sink with a hank of her hair in one fist and a pair of scissors in the other. She gave herself a menacing look in the mirror. For a moment nothing further happened. Then she let go of her hair and put the scissors down. She pushed her head close to the mirror, like she was trying to see past the flesh on her face. She looked into her own eyes. Then she looked at the mirror image of the boy, who was sitting on the toilet behind her with his pants down around his ankles. She grabbed a towel from the rack on the back of the door and wrapped it around herself. 'Can't a person get a little privacy around here?' she asked, tossing her hair as she went out of the bathroom.

The girl lies on the bed with one of the boy's journals. For a moment, she experiences an emotion that threatens to get away from her. Or to take her away from where she is. She can't quite gather it up, this feeling. Whenever she looks down at the journal and tries to read from it, the words float. They seem to be at a complete loss in terms of what they might mean to each other. They drift on the page like something she's hallucinating, rising slowly up and drifting away from each other, like cars leaving a party and going in different directions, including up, so maybe more like rockets leaving a party and going toward different planets. The girl is completely adrift among all these words. It's something in her that is lost, she knows, and it makes her afraid. The more she tries to read these words the boy has written, the further away the boy seems to get. But then it's her that's drifting away. She lifts her head and blinks in the bright light from the bedroom window. She falls over sideways onto the bed and drops her head down onto the boy's pillow. Her hair spreads out like sparkly thread.

Maybe the moon was out. Dick couldn't really remember. There could just as easily have been clouds obscuring the moon and stars. It wasn't raining – that much Dick could say for certain. And it was warm. The woman Dick was planning to marry was wearing short sleeves. 'What about the garden?' Dick asked. 'You just sort of set it up,' whispered the woman, 'and then it does what it needs to.' She smiled, but there was something dark behind her wide-eyed stare that made Dick afraid. 'And after you get it set up,' murmured the woman, 'you basically just watch it.' 'Like a god?' Dick whispered. The woman breathed. 'Maybe you have to water it once in a while,' she said. 'Like a rose garden?' Dick asked, pulling away to try to get a look at her face. 'Yes,' she said, 'just like a rose garden.'

To the girl, it seems as though the boy's words mean what they mean only so long as you believe that they might mean something, but as soon as you go from believing that they might mean something to believing you know what they mean, they stop meaning anything.

'Do you think it's weird what I write in my journals?' the boy asked the girl. He held up one of his journals. 'Not really,' said the girl. 'It's just stuff you make up. Making stuff up is weird, if you ask me, but the stuff you make up is no weirder than the stuff anybody else makes up, I don't think.' 'I try to make my characters likeable, but also a little bit despicable,' said the boy, 'so that people will think it's intriguing, and worthwhile to read about them.' 'What people?' asked the girl. 'Who's going to read your journals?' The boy looked down. 'You might read them,' he suggested. 'I guess,' said the girl. She looked thoughtful. 'Do you think you'll ever make up stuff about anyone other than Dick?' she asked. The boy raised his eyebrows, then lowered them again. 'I'd stop making up stuff about Dick in a second if I could,' he said. 'I hate him.' He looked at the girl. 'Just as much as you do,' he said. 'Probably more.' The girl didn't look like she believed him. 'But I can't seem to escape him,' said the boy. 'No matter how hard I try.'

One moment, the girl is standing by the kitchen counter, trying to pour water into the coffee maker; the next, she's sitting in the kitchen and it's already noon. The blinds are shut and she can't summon the energy to push her chair back and stand up from the table. She tries to understand what she is feeling, but it's like when you are a kid in kindergarten and you put all the colours of paint together, thinking how beautiful it is going to be, and you wind up getting brown.

It was morning. The boy had been reading to the girl from his journal. It was a story that didn't seem to involve Dick, which surprised the girl, because that was rare, but other than the fact that Dick hadn't yet made an appearance, the girl had no idea what the story was about. The boy was stumbling, reading a line or two, then stopping and looking up at the girl, then going back to the journal. He seemed to want to tell her something, like maybe he had a new girlfriend and he was going to be leaving her now to go and live with this woman he'd met at some bar he snuck out to nights when he said he was working late. The girl was feeling weepy when the boy interrupted her thoughts. 'I'm Dick,' he blurted out. The girl squeaked out a laugh. 'You're a dick all right,' she said, rubbing her cheeks under her eyes. The boy made a noise through his nose that might have been a laugh, but to the girl it sounded more like a cry for help. 'That's not what I mean,' said the boy. He made the weird noise again, then suddenly looked serious. 'I mean,' he said, 'I'm Dick.' He paused for emphasis. '*The* Dick,' he said. The girl tried to still her heart. 'The one in the stories?' she asked. 'Yes,' said the boy, sounding a little relieved, like this had been bothering him for a long time and he had finally got it off his conscience. The girl regarded him. She opened her mouth to say something, then closed it again.

The girl ran her finger along the map spread out in her lap. 'We still have a couple hours left till Kissimmee,' she said. 'I can't believe we decided to drive all the way to Kissimmee,' said the boy. 'For some reason, I'm regretting it.' The girl laughed. 'I'm with you on that one,' she said. She laughed some more. 'That's a funny name for a town, don't you think?' she said, still looking down at the map. 'If you take away an "i" and an "m" and an "e," you get "kiss me."' The boy smiled. 'It sounds like one of those old Italian gangster movies and the guy is saying, "Kiss-a-me, baby,"' said the girl. If they'd been at home, and he hadn't been driving, the boy might have kissed the girl just then. But instead he kept driving. There were a lot of other cars around, driving off in every direction. The trees seemed too close to the sides of the road. It felt like a jungle was rising up over them, waiting to come down suddenly and do something totally unexpected, like kill them maybe.

It takes the girl several trips to bring all the journals into the laundry room. She clears out the cupboard above the washer and sets the journals neatly on the shelves in the order she's numbered them. Then she locks the cupboard and takes the key up to the bedroom. She thinks about throwing the key in the garbage or dropping it into the river down in the ravine. In the end, she puts it in her jewellery box, which she also locks. She takes the little key for the jewellery box and puts it in a tiny Tupperware container, then puts the Tupperware container in the freezer. *That should do it*, she thinks.

Dick is mad at her for locking him away in the cupboard down-stairs. This is what pops into the girl's mind when she sees the seedy-looking man in the interview she's watching while she waits for her coffee to brew. Why is she getting so freaked out? *This isn't Dick*, she tells herself. She closes the laptop quickly, like she's trying to trap Dick in there, so he can't get out. Then she opens it a little and tries to peek in, like she's got hold of Pandora's box and can't stop herself from seeing what's inside. 'It's like my eyes were getting fucked by the light,' says the Dick look-alike. *It is Dick*, thinks the girl. She feels a pang of terror and snaps the laptop shut again. The guy looks just how she imagines Dick. She closes her eyes and opens the laptop again. 'I could see objects,' says the Dick look-alike, ' – trees, birds, cars, houses, people even – but at the same time everything was made of light. It was so bright.' *He even sounds like Dick*, the girl thinks. *But how would I know what Dick sounds like?* The girl opens her eyes. It's like Dick has jumped out of the boy's journals into this interview. It's like a nightmare.

SUMMER

It doesn't seem like it could matter much which way she goes along this road, the girl thinks, so she goes right. As soon as she starts moving again, she feels better. Which way she chooses to go is of no consequence, she realizes. This makes it difficult to decide which way to go. But it's also a relief because it removes any inhibition the girl might have about choosing one path over the other. She comes to another intersection. Again, she hesitates. *Which way?* She drops down onto the grass at the edge of the sidewalk. She watches a row of ants march past her feet. She feels the warmth of her arms where they curl around her legs. She rests her chin on her knees and blinks. The sun hovers behind her. Up ahead, a few clouds drift across the blue sky. She watches one small cloud morphing and shedding bits of itself as it goes along, until it is completely gone, torn apart by the wind.

The new god smiles. 'Do you live near here?' she asks. The girl turns her head and looks one way along the street, then turns it again and looks the other way. 'You look familiar,' the new god says. 'Do I know you?' The girl doesn't say anything. The new god raises her eyebrows. 'Doesn't the old God live in your garage?' she asks, tipping her head slightly, as though listening for some silent motive emanating from the girl's being. The girl starts to say something, then stops. She shrugs. 'Not anymore,' she says.

'I always thought that the girl and I should get married,' the boy told the cat. 'So, after going out for six years, I asked her.' The cat was lying on its side on the bed with a catnip toy between its front paws. The boy could hear the girl down in the kitchen opening cupboards and banging pots. 'By the time I asked her to marry me, it was like walking a path,' the boy continued. 'I could do it with my eyes closed.' He closed his eyes as if to demonstrate to the cat. 'Lately, though, the path has been growing over. I've had to take detours.' He looked out the window. 'Sometimes I come to believe that I'm lost in the forest. I sit on the bathroom floor and weep because I think I've lost her.' He looked down at his feet, then back up at the cat. The cat seemed to be asleep, the catnip toy still trapped between its paws. 'I haven't lost her, though,' said the boy. 'I know that now.' He laughed a humourless little laugh and gave the catnip toy a nudge. The cat pulled back on the toy with its paws but didn't open its eyes. 'It was always my own forest,' said the boy. 'My own trees.' He shook his head. 'The girl didn't even know it existed.' The boy stood up as if to leave, but then spoke once more, this time looking directly at the cat. 'If you keep your own forest a secret,' he said, 'you can't expect your wife to come in looking for you.'

The girl finds a notebook at the back of the fridge. She dangles it from her fingers like it's something expired, something gone rotten that will surely stink if she opens it. *Where did it come from?* she wonders. It's as though a chunk of the boy has been at the back of the fridge all this time going rotten, like the boy's been chopped up by a serial killer, and this is some spoiled piece of the boy's meat.

Light shot up from beneath the horizon and sprayed the undersides of the clouds that were floating above the lake. Dick was sitting in the sand beside his mother. He could feel the warmth of her skin. He could hear her heartbeat. But it might have been his own heartbeat. He stood. He wanted to look down at his mother, but it felt better to just think about looking down at her sitting in the sand. He could have stood there beside her with his eyes shut forever, but he decided to walk away. He could always go back. But the feeling of having his mother beside him got stronger as he walked away, so he kept on walking.

The cat lifts its head. It looks at the girl as though expecting something. The girl feels vaporous. The cat licks its front paw quickly, three times, then settles its chin onto its paws. Its eyes are not quite shut. It seems to be turning to smoke. Somewhere, a radio is going. A blanket lies grey and bilious over the girl, like another being stitched onto her body.

'Don't get me wrong, I'm glad to be back.' *What a dude*, thinks the girl. He's wearing skinny jeans and a cowboy hat. An unlit cigarette dangles from his lips. The girl is surprised he doesn't have a belt of bullets strapped across his chest. 'Okay if I smoke?' the dude asks, making the cigarette bounce in his mouth. The interviewer says something and the dude pulls out a lighter, flicks it, then holds the flame to the tip of the cigarette. He squints and the cigarette flares. He snaps the lighter shut. The girl thinks about turning the interview off. It's not like this dude is going to tell her something she doesn't already know. *Why do I keep watching these?* she asks herself, even as she continues to watch. The dude is standing by a lamppost outside a convenience store on a busy street in a city somewhere. Traffic on the street behind him is crawling. Storm clouds are gathering in the distance. 'But at the time,' dude says, 'I didn't mind being where I was.' He pulls on the cigarette, holds the smoke a moment, then breathes it out. It hovers briefly around his head, then gets whisked away by the wind. He seems completely oblivious to the storm moving closer behind him as he speaks. 'It wasn't like I'd been taken away,' dude says. 'At least, it didn't feel like that.' He shrugs. 'It was more like a subtle shift in my state of mind. But also like I had no mind. So, how could I mind this new state of mind?' He shrugs. 'I had no mind to state it in.' He takes another drag on the cigarette. The girl watches the smoke drift from his nose. It makes her want to have a cigarette. She's never smoked. She's always thought it disgusting. It would make her breath stink. And her clothes. Plus it could kill you. But none of that seems to matter much now. She's old and who does she have to smell good for? Maybe the cat wouldn't like it, though. 'I mean,' says the dude, 'it felt like I had one.' He holds his cigarette up, like he's proffering it to the camera. 'A mind, I mean. Or maybe it was more like I had a mind, but it wasn't *my* mind.' He nods. 'Yeah,' he says, 'it was like having somebody else's mind.' The interviewer says something. Dude turns back, sucks on the cigarette, blows out smoke. 'The other guy is still there inside me,' he says. 'I can feel him there.' The girl sits back in her chair. 'I mean, sometimes I can feel him there,' dude says. 'Other times, I can't feel him at all. And I miss him.' The interview fades. If the boy were ever to come back, the girl realizes, he'd have another guy inside him, too, and that other guy would be Dick. The boy's other guy is Dick. It was always Dick.

The girl can feel herself drifting off. She thinks she hears the boy's voice, like a beam of light stabbing through a cloud, touching her on the heart. The boy is a dream, beamed out of the girl's head, through her eyes. Her eyes are the lenses on a projector and the boy is her movie. In the movie, the girl is far ahead of the boy, walking away from him along a beach, the sun a big red ball dropping below the horizon on the other side of the lake. The girl is moving forward, looking over her shoulder at the boy, beckoning him to come along, but only if he wants. The boy stays standing still, his arms hanging useless at his sides. The girl wants to go back and console him. Or punch him. Or hold him and wipe away his tears. But she keeps moving, feeling the jagged edge of his shrinking away from her like a knife blade gently scoring her skin.

The girl wakes up. She goes to the window. The room smells nice. The grass next door has been mown. It's sunny. The shades rattle in the breeze that's blowing in where the girl has opened the window a little. The slats of the blinds create horizontal intersections, making the room look like a photo that has been folded into a fan, then opened again. A cardinal lands on the branch of a tree, bright red in the morning sun. The girl dips her head to see it better through the slots in the blinds.

Sometimes, the girl still believes she can feel the presence of the boy, like he's coming back to her. But it isn't him, it's like a phantom limb, something the girl has agreed to have amputated but can't quite get rid of. In the kitchen, or in the basement, or in the bedroom, she feels something like an itch. It's like he's over by the window, looking out, and where he is isn't exactly where he is, but more where he's looking. And the reason the girl can't see him now is because he wants to be where he's looking, not where he is, so that where he is is never where he is but always where he's looking. If she goes to where the boy used to stand by the window and looks where the boy used to look, will she be able to see him? Is he where he always wanted to be when he stood by the window looking out? If so, why should he come back? Why would the girl even want him to come back?

It's August. The girl is sitting on a bench in the park. God arrives in her 1965 red-and-white Mustang convertible.

The girl is not a fool. Nor is the boy, she understands. In her most empty moments, at the point when she surrenders so completely that it feels like release, the girl knows with absolute certainty that it doesn't matter whether or not the boy comes back, because he will always be there with her, and he will always, even and most particularly when he is standing right in front of her, be gone. This thing of him disappearing is just a new way of seeing the boy.

The air is quite cool for September. The boy has been gone for nearly a year. It would have been his birthday today. The leaves in the tree outside the kitchen window look like giant yellow teardrops frozen to branches of the sun.

A young woman sits at a table. Behind her is a kitchen sink with a window above it. The sun is shining through the window. The woman's got a mug of coffee, or it could be tea, sitting on the table in front of her, with a bit of steam rising from it. It's a terrible angle to film the woman from, and the girl wants to hate the interviewer for this new form of incompetence, but having the light behind the woman actually seems to work. The girl likes the way the light from behind makes it look like the woman has a halo. 'It felt like it was too far to go to come back,' says the haloed woman. She's staring into the distance, as though seeing the place she was when she didn't think she was coming back. 'It was like I had someplace to go, but the place I had to go was back to where I was and I didn't quite know if I wanted to come back to where I was, although I could see that even if I did come back to exactly where I already was I would be in a different place from where I was before I disappeared, even if it was the same place I have always been.' She looks down. Her hair is yellow in the sunlight. 'Where did you have to go?' the interviewer prompts when the woman doesn't seem about to say anything more, and for some reason, the girl can make out very clearly what the interviewer is saying. In fact, the distant deadness of the interviewer's voice seems perfect in contrast to the woman's intimately voiced musicality. The woman looks at the interviewer like she's looking at a friend, and the girl can't help feeling befriended. 'I don't know,' says the woman. A smile plays across her face. 'I can't remember,' she says. Her eyes shine like pools of dark liquid. 'Fuck,' she says, but it's a gentle 'fuck.' 'Sorry,' she says, her eyes alight with mischief. 'Can you bleep that out?' she asks, grinning crookedly. 'It's okay,' says the interviewer, 'I want you to be candid.' The woman laughs a little and her hair seems to tremble. 'It doesn't matter now, anyway,' she says. 'It isn't possible to be where I needed to be.' 'And where is it you needed to be?' the interviewer persists. The woman shrugs. She bites her lip. 'When I try now to think where I needed to be then, it's like I don't need to be anywhere ever again. It feels good. While I was gone, there was something deep in the back of my mind that was telling me it wasn't good. But then it was like the front of my mind was laughing at the back of my mind, like, don't be stupid, just enjoy this.' She picks up her mug and holds it for a moment, then puts it back down without drinking from it. 'It's like being in a warm taxi on a wet night,' she says with a sort of happy vacancy in her eyes. 'You know how taxis always have that stale smell that's faintly disgusting,' she says. 'But you're warm in the back of the taxi.' She smiles right at the camera, and the girl feels like she's in the taxi with this woman, like they're a couple of little kids holding hands, going on a trip together without their parents. 'And the driver asks you where you want to go,' says the haloed woman, 'and you tell him, "Just drive. Just keep driving forever."'

FALLING

'I'm not accusing you,' says the boy. But it isn't the boy. It's the girl. She's talking to herself. She pulls her sweater tight around her and looks down. Even the cat looks like it's accusing her. She bats a piece of hair away from her face. She thinks she hears voices. *They must be outside,* she thinks. A small black letter appears on the kitchen counter, soon to be joined by another, and then another, until the counter is crowded with them. At first they look like toast crumbs, spread haphazardly around, and the girl wants to get the dishcloth and wipe them away. But then they gather together, like they are trying to reform into a new piece of toast, but they can't do it, because … The girl tries to think. Well … because it can't be done. You can't form a new piece of toast from the crumbs of an old one. The girl feels like she's figured something out, something important. She feels important. The cat looks at her like she's important. 'Accuse that,' she says to the boy. *What is this?* she thinks. Does she want to accuse the boy of something? And if so, is this the best she can manage, accusing the boy of accusing her? She wishes she could accuse him of something more substantial.

The girl is inside the boy, swimming. The boy expands. The hole in the world yawns wider under the girl as she pushes out toward the void. A bus pulls up. The girl gets on. The first snowflakes of the winter drift by on the wind. Inside the bus, it's warm and it smells like kerosene. The girl hears the whoosh of angel wings. She looks up from her cereal. The cat is standing very still on the window ledge, looking up at the sky. The girl feels the boy slipping away. He disappears like this almost every morning, only to reappear again later in the day like an errant parent, showing up once a week to tell her everything will be okay.

The girl can feel the boy playing hopscotch inside her body. He's touching her from inside, like reaching out from her bowels, peering out through her navel, like it's a peephole on a door. She hears the echo of birds calling her name from outside. She sits up suddenly and finds herself alone. *At least I've found myself,* she thinks. She wonders if that's a good thing. 'I feel like you want too much from me,' she mumbles. *But nobody wants anything from me,* she thinks. She tries to remember where she is. Something drifts by, close to her face, like a memory, or a fist, or a vision, or an angel, or maybe just a smell.

There is something she should have been telling the boy all along, the girl thinks, but now it's too late. Even if he ever does come back, it is always going to be too late, because nothing is his fault anymore now that he is gone. But what is it she was going to tell him anyway? What would be the use of telling him anything? 'Tie your shoes'? 'Eat your soup before it gets cold'? 'I love you'? Whatever she says to him, now, or before, or whenever, it's always going to be too late. Because whatever it is that she wants to set down between them is something that was always already there between them, floating in the air like a bad smell that needs to be destroyed by something pine-scented. The girl turns sideways in her chair. 'I want to tell you something,' she says to the boy, even though she knows he isn't really there. 'I kind of like taking care of myself,' she says. 'I'm sorry about that,' she adds, feeling something infiltrate her body, like pee filling her bladder.

Taking a bite of her toast, the girl closes her eyes. She feels the boy give her back her heart. She hears him in the beating emptiness of her bloodstream. *When I picture you,* the boy whispers from where he's hovering, fading slowly away inside her head, *I picture horses disappearing into a field where only horses can go.* But it's him that's disappearing. The girl leans back into this new vision of the boy. She can feel his fingers linger in her hair. *How big is death?* she asks sleepily. When the boy doesn't answer, she sits up straight and takes another bite of her toast.

Morning sun blasts the few remaining leaves on the right sides of trees, slaps the faces of westbound drivers, and lights up one side of the girl's hair. It shoots over the tops of low buildings and hacks off the tops of taller buildings on the other side of the street. It hides behind the bandshell in the park. It feels to the girl as though the space she exists in is a walk-in freezer full of frozen moments that keep getting ripped out of her life. And then the freezer tips over onto its side and the moments crack and lie broken where they have fallen, and the girl is bobbing about the sea of her life unconstrained by chronology, a tiny cork on the waves of the incoming moment. She wants to become something else, something beyond what she has surely already become. Sometimes she thinks she can see the boy, like the ghostly reflection you glimpse in a window at night. He speaks to her as though through a door, from a place she can't enter. She can barely make him out, no matter how hard she tries, and sometimes she doesn't even try.

The girl feels something enter her like an alien presence. It talks to her. It tries to tell her what to do. It tells her: *Stop! Stop doing this to yourself.* It talks to her in the boy's voice. But then the voice isn't the boy's voice and the words aren't words. It's just a lot of noise inside the girl's head. She opens her eyes. She's alone. She's pretty sure she's still in the bedroom, but if it is the bedroom, it's not the same bedroom she once occupied with the boy.

The girl dreams she is lying under a picnic table in the cold, looking at stars through the slats of the tabletop. Someone is talking to her. She decides it must be the boy. The boy must be up there somewhere in the night sky. She wakes to the feeling she isn't real. She looks down at her body sheathed in a gauzy nightgown. She imagines her breasts as hills, the nipples like tiny brown huts. The dome of her belly rolls down into the valley where her legs emerge from her trunk and then travel in two separate directions, as though trying to get away from each other. She can feel herself unravelling. She pulls on gloves. She can see her breath in the morning sun. Suddenly everything makes perfect sense. Across the road in the fields, birds fly up out of the dying grass. It hurts to understand.

Bright light ripped from blue sky conjures trees, people, roadways, buildings. The girl tries to move forward. *I'm not sure how much longer I can do this,* she thinks, trying to reel in a fish. But they aren't fish. They're clouds. And she isn't doing anything but walking. And she isn't even doing that. The girl awakes to find herself swimming through an array of variants, each of which presents itself as this or that, even as they all fall out of their own peculiarity awash in colourless sound and light. The next-door neighbour is mowing her lawn. An oily smell like boats idling in the marina drifts in through the kitchen window, assaulting the girl where she sits at the kitchen table in a black T-shirt and pink panties. With her eyes closed, the girl can see the shadow of something she believes she's conjured in her mind. She realizes that her eyes are still slightly open and the shadows she's seeing are the outlines of things that actually exist.

The girl is in the hammock on the porch when the angel comes and tells her to hush. 'Be quiet now,' says the angel. The girl sleeps. When she wakes, the angel is nothing but a streak of sunlight burnt into her eyeball. *The inside of the boy's head is like a hallway. He just can't find his way into the right room.* The girl crosses the river. She can feel the boy moving in the bed beside her. She keeps her eyes closed and doesn't say anything. *I smoked another cigarette and conferred with the woman,* the boy says. *What woman?* thinks the girl. But she doesn't speak. *The woman told me we could not keep on the way we were going,* says the boy. *I winched up my pack, threw it over my back, then just stood there. 'The time to leave is now,' said the woman.* And sure enough, when the girl opens her eyes, the boy is gone.

The girl falls. She falls and falls, like a waterfall with no river below it. Above her, wind tortures clouds, tearing them apart slowly, piece by piece, until there is nothing left but the blood-red sun descending below the horizon. God is there wearing a hat. 'Hello, God,' says the girl. 'Hello,' says God, 'what's your name?' God watches her. 'Do I know you?' God asks. The girl has no idea how to answer. She shrugs, then steps into the security line at the airport. She finds herself standing on a precipice watching a plane fly by. She's high enough up to see the faces of the passengers through the little round windows on the side of the plane. The plane is silent. It makes no noise as it disappears into clouds. The girl walks out across the clouds to follow it. She finds herself back down at the bottom of the mountain, sitting in her little home in the valley where she lives with her goats. She has her eyes closed. She hears footsteps. God is coming along the sidewalk toward her, wearing some kind of hard-soled shoes. The girl arrives with the feeling she is late for something, like rain spilling endlessly down the sides of buildings, over streets, through the gutters, trying to get back to where she thought she was going before she fell from the sky. Inside the girl's closet, there are many colourful outfits waiting.

When the girl runs her fingers through her hair, it tumbles about her shoulders like dead snakes shuddering back to life, falling dead again when she takes away her hands. Outside, birds tear past beneath the clouds and vanish. In the emptiness following their departure, flakes of snow drift by on the wind. A plane flies past high above, looking like a phantom image projected onto clouds. On the gentle hill that she is descending, in the foothills of a mountain she can no longer see, the girl finds herself wanting to get back out onto flat land. She wants to get far enough away from this hill so that she can turn back and see the mountains again. Downstairs at the dryer, the girl realizes she didn't pause the TV.

The girl stumbles on the edge of a cliff, then falls into a white-water canyon where words scramble about like music lost down a subway tunnel. She can't quite catch the tune as she tries to get her head above water. She can hear bits of music, like the echo of some creature blown apart in a cavern, trying to put itself back together, dragging its own bloody carcass through the dark, searching for parts of itself that it doesn't yet understand are gone forever. The girl tries to remember something the boy once said to her. She tries to hear his voice. She closes her eyes, tilts her head back. On the insides of her eyelids, she sees the bright outline of the window she was looking out before she tried to remember the boy. But the boy is a wind that has torn the girl to pieces, something violent and unseen.

The girl wakes driving to the bakery. She holds the wheel, turns it when necessary. She passes a gas station. A restaurant. She stops under a billboard with a picture of a tattooed woman. There's a cloud of cigarette smoke frozen by the camera near the woman's face. A door shuts in the night, waking the girl. At seven-thirty, the garbage truck comes whining into the girl's dreams like sunlight infiltrating a forest. *The boy is the buzz in my ears*, thinks the girl, *like something I've always known as God, but only because I don't know what else to call it*. She opens her eyes, then blinks, the sunlight slashing through her eyelashes like wheat through the teeth of a thresher.

Late at night, the house is silent. The girl listens for rain hitting the window, for wind, for birdsong, for the boy. The covers lie across the bed like clouds seen from above. Like a blanket for the sky. The girl wakes. She has seen the boy. He's in a place that has no dimensions. He is nothing, an amorphous shape, an empty space. She reaches out toward him, feels herself tipping, then falling, then whirling around. And then the girl becomes the empty space she's been falling through, disappearing into what was once the boy.

PART 2

The boy returns on a cold morning in October, more than a year after he disappeared. The girl is not surprised to see him through the peephole when he knocks on the door. The internet has prepared her. 'You don't have your key?' she asks as she opens the door. 'I didn't take it,' he says. 'I didn't know I was going anywhere,' he adds. 'Where did you go, anyway?' asks the girl. 'I don't know,' says the boy. This doesn't surprise the girl either.

Something wakes the girl. Someone is banging around in the kitchen. 'Is that the boy?' the girl whispers to the cat. Early-morning light sneaks in through the window blinds. The cat cleans its whiskers. The girl rubs her face. She puts her hands on the sides of her head. Her hair feels terrible, like she's slept on it. *I have slept on it*, she thinks with a startled laugh. She puts her legs over the edge of the bed. Downstairs, a spoon clinks in a bowl. *That's a cereal bowl*, thinks the girl. She stands. Gets her bathrobe off the back of the bedroom door. Puts it on. She peeks out into the hall, then turns back to look at the cat. 'Call the police if I'm not back in five minutes,' she stage-whispers, putting her hand to the side of her mouth. Then she slips out of the room. She stands at the top of the stairs. She can hear the boy talking to himself in the kitchen. She goes down the stairs. The house is bright. The boy has turned on all the lights. He's stirring something in a bowl. The oven is preheating. 'What are you making?' the girl asks. 'It doesn't matter,' says the boy. Something fills the girl's chest. 'You need to see past all that,' says the boy without looking up. 'You need to see past the recipe.' The girl steps back. 'How can I do that?' she asks. She feels as though her insides are dissolving like butter melting in a pot. 'To see past the recipe,' says the boy, still stirring vigorously away at whatever he is stirring, 'you must engender a kind of synthesis of attention and abuse.' Now he looks up from the bowl and gazes at the girl pointedly. 'You have to go into your recipe archive,' he says, 'without any predetermined ideas about what you'll get out of it.' He's stopped stirring at some point and now he looks back into the bowl and pulls his head back a little. 'Whoa,' he says, as though he's seen the meaning of the universe in his bowl. He shrugs and goes back to stirring. He is in his boxers and a black T-shirt and his feet are bare. His hair is neatly brushed. 'You can use the My Recipes tab of the Your Chatelaine magazine website to try to examine your relationship to what you eat.' He looks at the girl again. 'You need to fix your hair,' he tells her, pointing his eyes upward toward his own hair. The oven beeps to say that it has reached the desired temperature. 'Try to understand the relationship between yourself and your recipes,' the boy says. 'Try to discover the ingredients of what might make you into what you need yourself to be.' The girl nods. This actually makes sense.

The girl looks up from where she's sitting over a piece of toast. 'Good morning,' she says. 'Hi,' says the boy, 'I'm looking for something.' His hair sticks up at the back. He tugs on the waist of his pyjama bottoms, which are hanging off him like a flag with no wind. 'Did I have some notebooks?' he asks. He looks forlorn. The girl gets up from the table and goes over to stand before him. She puts her hands on his arms. *He really isn't sure,* she thinks. This seems inconceivable. 'Wait,' she says. She goes to the freezer, gets out the Tupperware container with the key to her jewellery box in it, and goes upstairs. The boy stays where he is in the middle of the kitchen. When the girl returns, she takes the boy by the hand and leads him down to the basement. She unlocks the cupboard over the dryer and opens it so the boy can see his journals, lined up neatly on three shelves, one above the other. The boy looks even more lost. 'I keep them down here?' he asks, staring at the journals. 'Locked in a cupboard?' He turns to the girl. The girl thinks about telling him yes, this is where he has always kept them. And he would believe her. He trusts her, she understands. He's alone in the world except for her. Maybe in spite of her. 'No,' she says. 'I locked them up down here after you disappeared.' She reaches up and pulls one out. 'I numbered them, see.' She holds it out to the boy. He takes it but doesn't open it. Just stands where he is, looking down, holding the journal in both hands, like he's caressing it. 'Of course, I have no idea what order you made them in,' the girl says. 'They were all over the house. I think I found this one in the cereal cupboard.' She laughs. The boy manages a smile. He looks down at the journal. Opens it. For a moment, the girl thinks he might read to her from it, like he used to. But then he closes it and looks at the girl. 'Thanks,' he says. 'Do you think I could get a piece of that toast you were having?' The girl draws her head back a little. 'Sure,' she says with a wary little smile. 'You want anything on it?' she asks. 'Just butter,' says the boy.

Dick can't figure out what exactly it is he is looking at. It's late afternoon and he's just got back to the cabin after going into town to get lunch. He couldn't decide what to buy for lunch, so he didn't buy anything, and now he's hungry. He stands in the cabin looking out the front window. He looks at the sunset. He looks at the lake. He looks at the tall grass rising up out of the dunes. He sees all these things, but it's like he's blind to a certain colour, a colour he can decipher only through context. And he can't seem to gather any context anymore.

The girl comes into the bedroom and finds the boy sitting on the edge of the bed. He looks tired. His hair sticks out in every direction. He's wearing one of the girl's T-shirts, but he has it on inside out. The girl takes his hand. She leads him out of the bedroom and down the stairs. She sits him down in his chair at the kitchen table. 'What's going on?' asks the boy, rubbing his face. 'I've been working on a new recipe,' says the girl. She gets out a slice of bread and puts it in the toaster. Then she gets out the jar of mayonnaise and a tin of tuna and sets them on the counter. She sits down across from the boy and the two of them wait for the toast to cook.

It's dark. The boy lifts his phone to see what time it is. He can hear the girl moving around upstairs in the bedroom. He sets his phone back down on the coffee table. He listens to his heart.

'I'm going to need some olive oil,' the boy tells the cat as he drifts back to sleep. In his dream, Dick stands at the stove, stirring something in a pot, while the cat stands behind him, whispering secrets about the girl.

Suddenly, out of nowhere, a word appears. It seems to have fallen from the sky, although they don't see it fall. It's just there, after having not been there. It sits squarely in the middle of the road. They can make out individual letters, but they can't put them together. 'What does it say?' asks the boy. 'I don't know,' says the girl, 'I can't read it.' Her face catches the light coming in through the living room window, making her cheeks look like twin moons. 'Maybe it doesn't say anything,' says the boy.

The boy sprays words across the bedroom, like water bursting from a pipe. The girl reaches over the edge of the bed to pick up something she's dropped. When the boy looks back down at the book he's holding in his lap, he finds he's lost his desire to read to the girl. He looks up again and the girl's eyes are closed. Her lips are slightly open. She has a look on her face that the boy wants to interpret as longing. She's moving her lips a little, but if she's saying anything, the boy can't make it out. He watches her fall asleep. He knows she is sound asleep by the way she breathes, her chest rising and falling slowly. He leans over her to look at her face, which looks like release. Her breath smells of hunger. It seems to the boy that she must have, at some point while he was gone, given up eating. She looks so skinny. He gets out of the bed carefully, trying not to wake her. He stands by the bed not moving, just watching the girl. When he finally gets up the courage to move, he tries to time his steps to the girl's breathing. He makes it out into the hall without waking her. He closes the door softly. 'Dick stood in the dark hall for a long time,' he whispers, 'trying to remember what his mother looked like.'

The girl is standing at the sink, drinking water from her favourite glass. The boy is sitting at the kitchen counter, reading aloud from the screen of his laptop. Above them, the overhead fan whirs. In his mind, the boy is forty years younger, standing with the girl by a river, watching his baseball cap get swept away downstream after the wind blows it off his head.

The sky grows dark as they sit together on the beach. There is something coming across the water toward them, but it's too far away to see what it is. Dick turns to see if his mother looks afraid. She doesn't. She looks calm. Dick isn't sure if he himself feels afraid. He thinks he might. Dick's mother looks over at Dick for a time, then she pats him on the knee. 'Don't be afraid,' she says.

'Pause it,' says the girl. The boy stops the movie. 'I have to get some chocolate,' says the girl. She goes upstairs. The boy sits still, like a character on TV waiting for someone to unpause him.

The girl and the boy decide to take a nap together. They go up to the bedroom. The girl needs to keep a glass of water by the bed in case she suddenly gets thirsty. She puts on some lip balm. The boy takes his shirt off, otherwise he gets too hot. He pulls back the bedcovers. The cat jumps up on the bed and lies down in the middle of it. 'How does it get its body to take up so much bed?' asks the girl. She pushes the cat over to the boy's side and proceeds to move her pillows around, getting them in position for the nap. The boy looks down at the cat while the girl gets her pillows ready. After the girl is in the bed and settled among her pillows, the boy slides the cat down to the end of the bed and gets in. The cat looks at the boy like it would kill him if it had the energy. It puts its head down on its paws but keeps an eye on the boy. The boy curls up on the edge of the bed with the feeling that he might at any moment fall off it to his death.

'I'm not sure how much longer I can lie here,' says the boy. He's on his back in the bed with the covers up to his chin. 'That's okay,' says the girl. 'I have to pee now anyway.' She takes her hand off the boy's chest and slips out from under the bedcovers. The boy watches her go into the bathroom, his mind still lingering in a space he believes he can one day inhabit fully if only he can locate it more precisely.

After the boy leaves in the morning, the girl sits quietly at the kitchen table in her white nightie, staring out the window. The boy drives across town and goes into a diner, where he orders bacon and eggs and a cup of coffee. He sits at the counter. The woman who serves him smiles as she takes his order. They make small talk. Pretty soon, the boy's breakfast arrives. When he gets back home in the early afternoon, the boy hands the girl a large takeout coffee. It's ice cold. The girl, who is sitting at the kitchen table right where the boy left her when he went out to get his breakfast, looks up at the boy like he's someone with special needs that she can't meet.

Dick's back hurts. And then after a while it doesn't hurt. Dick is running. Then he's on a bus. He's reading. He realizes that his back has stopped hurting. He says, 'Thank you,' quietly to his back and puts his book away. He likes that the pain is gone, but also, it has been a sort of companion. It's as though the pain is a friend who has moved out of Dick's back into a new apartment just down the street. Dick wants to pay attention now to the suddenly quiet space that the pain previously occupied. So he stops reading and just sits. Someone gets off the bus. Dick burps. His face looks like a statue.

The boy hears a small sound and looks up to see the girl coming into the living room. He smiles. She stares at him. His eyes look too bright. 'It's like you suddenly just occurred to me,' he says. 'Like I conjured you out of nothing.' He laughs like someone who needs a haircut and knows it but doesn't do anything about it because he's gone mad.

'If you imagine yourself to be what you aren't,' murmurs the girl, looking up from a deep sleep, 'it's quite possible that you might wind up being someone you never were.' The boy emerges from her dream as she drifts back into sleep. He doesn't want to disturb her. He whispers into her ear, hoping he can send his words directly into her dream. The girl is his dream, and he is only this stream of words he is pulsing into her, like blood entering a heart.

The boy is writing in the new journal he started shortly after he returned. The girl comes into the bedroom with coffees. She sets them on the bedside table. She gets into bed beside the boy. 'What are you writing?' she asks, nodding at the journal. The boy reaches past the girl and gets his coffee. 'Can I read it?' asks the girl. The boy takes a sip of his coffee and looks down at his journal. 'I guess so,' he says. He makes no move to hand the journal to the girl. The girl waits, then reaches over for the journal. 'Is this about Dick?' she asks. The boy has his cup halfway to his mouth. 'I'm not sure,' he says through the steam from his coffee. He puts the cup to his lips. 'What do you mean,' asks the girl, 'don't you know what you're writing about?' 'No,' says the boy, 'not really.' He sets his cup down. 'I mean,' he says, 'it isn't about Dick per se. But sometimes I think everything is about Dick. It's like Dick is always there, chasing me, and I can't get away.'

'When I was a kid,' says the girl, 'someone from the furnace company put the wrong kind of fuel in our fuel tank and the furnace caught fire. We had to run out of the house in our pyjamas.' The girl shakes her head, smiling at the memory. 'I can still picture my mother standing in the street in her pyjamas, holding one of the cats in her arms, rocking it gently like it was her baby. Her face looked so beautiful lit by the fire of our burning house.' 'You have a mother?' asks the boy. The girl looks at the boy, startled. 'Of course,' she says. The boy says nothing. Then he says, 'I didn't think you would have a mother.' 'Really?' asks the girl. She looks worried. 'Where did you think I came from?' she asks. 'I didn't think you came from anywhere,' says the boy. 'I thought you were always here.'

At seven o'clock the phone rings. The walls are white with blue lines. Bunches of lilac blossom in the garden. The boy turns and walks through a doorway. He finds himself in April. The girl stands before him like wind in his empty mind. When he returns, he shuts the door behind him. 'I want to go back there sometime,' he whispers to himself.

The boy is sitting on the stairs, untying his shoes. The girl is behind him, looking down at the top of his head. 'There was a man at work today who said he had never heard the word *kid*,' says the boy. He waits for the girl to say something, but she doesn't. 'He asked me what it meant,' the boy continues. 'I tried to tell him.' He hesitates. 'I knew what *kid* meant, of course.' He looks away from the girl, into the air in front of him, hands still on his shoelaces. 'But I could not, for the life of me,' he says, 'find a way to tell this man what I knew.'

The boy wakes up. He's in his bed at home. The girl is sitting at her vanity, sorting through her earrings. The boy turns his head to look out the window. The sun shines on his face. He closes his eyes. The girl feels like she should maybe go over and sit on the bed with him. Maybe touch him. Hold him. Love him. But she doesn't think she wants to touch him. Or maybe it isn't so much that she doesn't want to touch him, more that she doesn't want to fall into the hole she knows she will fall into if she does touch him.

When the girl comes down to the kitchen to get some coffee, she finds the boy waiting for her. He has some news. He takes the girl by both hands and looks her in the eye. 'My heart's still beating,' he says. The girl waits. 'That's it?' she says. She waits and waits and waits. But the boy doesn't say anything else, just lifts the girl's hands to his chest and holds them there.

The woman at the door is small, thin. 'I'm here for the interview,' she says. The girl pulls her head back, confused. The boy told her he was being interviewed – but this can't be the interviewer. The interviewer is a guy. She looks closer at the woman. *Maybe this is a different interviewer*, she thinks. *Or the interviewer's assistant. Would he even have an assistant?* the girl wonders. *And if he does have an assistant, wouldn't he have hired someone who knows how to work a microphone?* 'Are you okay?' asks the woman. The girl looks up. 'I thought you were a guy,' she says. The woman laughs. 'I've watched all your interviews on YouTube,' says the girl. 'I thought you were a guy.' The woman laughs some more. 'It's probably the ad,' she says. 'Did you see the ad?' The girl nods. 'That's my husband,' says the interviewer. 'He's the brains behind this operation.' She looks at the girl pointedly. 'I just follow orders,' she says with a gruff snort. The girl sits in the living room during the interview. The interviewer is in the kitchen with her camera set up at one end of the table and the boy sitting at the other. Now that she's hearing it like this, from a distance, the girl realizes this woman's voice is the same as the one from the interviews. The girl rattles her head a little, as if trying to get water out of her ear. 'Since I've been back,' the boy tells the interviewer, 'it feels like a great willow is dripping its leafy tears onto me, like a magnificent pillow of soft sadness is overlaying my face and heart. And I am breathing through the thickness of this pillow of sadness.' In the living room, the cat jumps onto the girl's lap and makes a tiny mewling sound, as though it's not sure what's happening and is pretty certain it doesn't like it. 'And in the middle of the night,' says the boy from the kitchen, 'when I put my actual pillow over my face to cover the brightness of my eyes that shine like lonely beacons in the dark, I am afraid that I am going to disappear again.' The cat pushes its nose into the girl's hand. The interviewer says something to the boy. The girl realizes with a start that it isn't just the way the interviews are miked that makes it impossible to understand what the interviewer is saying. It's something about the way she pitches her voice, like she's got something to hide, or she doesn't want to be heard. 'Well, yes,' says the boy in response to what the interviewer has asked, 'maybe sometimes. It was so easy there. Or … not exactly easy. More like … I don't know … it wasn't easy or hard … more like there was nothing that could qualify as easy or hard.' It's quiet for a moment, then the boy says: 'But I don't know if I'd actually want to go back.' He laughs. 'Anyway, I'd want to take my wife with me if I did.' He laughs again, a little nervously to the girl's ear. The interviewer says something, and again the girl can't make it out. 'Yes,' says the boy, 'I think she'd like it there. Definitely. I mean, who wouldn't?'

'When I was in Grade 4, I did a story about a time machine.' The boy is sitting with God by the tiny indoor pool at the Super 8 hotel where God is staying. 'I've got the honeymoon suite,' God says, leaning forward in her plastic lounger to grin at the boy. 'Funny, right?' she says. 'They've got a honeymoon suite at this dump?' asks the boy, looking around like a turtle that's sorry it stuck its head out of its shell. 'I know,' says God, sitting back again in her lounger and closing her eyes. 'It's crazy.' She takes a sip of her soda and sighs. 'The story I wrote was about a kid who built a time machine in his spare time after school and went places in it,' says the boy. God's head lolls toward the boy. The boy does his best not to look down her bikini top. 'I like science fiction,' God says in a voice that's a mix between sultry and asleep. The boy doesn't say anything. 'Where did the boy in the story go?' God asks lazily. 'I can't really remember where he went, or any of the specifics,' says the boy. God says, 'Probably back to the 1800s, right? Or to the time of the dinosaurs.' She lets out a little laugh. 'That's where everybody sends their characters in time machine stories.' She pauses, then adds energetically: 'Did the kid step on a butterfly?' She laughs some more. 'I love stories where the protagonist steps on a butterfly and changes all of history so that her own world is a dystopian nightmare when she returns. Then she spends the rest of the story trying to make things right.' The boy doesn't say anything. Then he says, 'The thing I really remember about that story was it got four stars.' He looks at God to gauge her reaction, but God says nothing, doesn't move, doesn't even open her eyes. 'The teacher used to stick these stars on our stories,' says the boy. 'One star if the story sucked. Two if it was okay. Three if it was great. But no one ever got four stars. That was the most stars you could get.' The boy looks over at God, who still has her eyes closed. 'Are you even listening?' the boy asks. 'I'm listening,' God says. 'Don't you get it?' says the boy, sitting up in his lounger and turning toward God. 'Everyone was amazed that I got four stars.' 'That is pretty amazing,' God says. She takes another sip of her soda. 'You should have one of these sodas,' she says. 'They're really good.'

The girl sits atop the orange rug, alone in the basement, her face pinched, as though she is at the bottom of a deep lake, running out of time, looking up every second or so to check the gauge on her oxygen tank.

When the boy wakes up, it's morning. He decides to go down to the kitchen. Make some coffee. When the girl gets up an hour later, she sits at the kitchen table, eyes closed, fidgeting with her hands. She is wearing her white nightie and her feet are bare. The boy scrambles eggs and sings. He adds peanut butter to the eggs. 'Excuse me,' says the girl. The boy takes his hand off the handle of the frying pan. 'Did you just put peanut butter in my eggs?' The boy looks down at the frying pan, then turns to look at the girl. 'Maybe,' he says, watching her face.

The girl is leaning in close to the mirror over the bathroom sink, tweezing something on her face. The boy comes up behind her and puts his hands on her shoulders. The girl stops tweezing. She seems to be shaking. The boy can feel her trembling up through her core into his arms, like she's sending him a telegraph message from far away.

'I remember everything,' says the boy. 'But I can't say what I remember.' The interviewer is back. It's the third time she's interviewed the boy. 'What I mean,' says the boy, 'is that it isn't hard to remember what happened, because it all happened at once, like a single memory. A lot happened, but it all happened in a single moment.' The boy has been staring out the window, but now he looks directly at the interviewer. She nods encouragingly. 'Above me is this giant stack of moments,' says the boy, 'moments that have completely lost their character as moments.' His speech is hesitant. 'Each moment,' he says, 'has become just another instance of now.' He lifts his hands. 'I can't move forward.' He drops his hands. 'I'm not a story,' he says. His voice is quiet. The interviewer nods again, as though she understands. 'We have scaled the heights of nothing,' says the boy, 'and now we find ourselves contingent.' He shrugs and picks up his coffee. He lifts it to his lips, takes a sip, sets the cup back down. He stares out the window. 'Contingent on what?' asks the interviewer. The boy continues to stare out the window. 'Contingent,' he says, speaking the word as though he has to stick his finger down his throat to get it out, 'on … ' he darts his eyes about, then drops his shoulders, 'nothing,' he says finally. He shrugs helplessly. 'We're contingent on nothing,' he repeats. At this moment, the girl comes into the kitchen and both the interviewer and the boy look up at her as though they've been living together alone in a quonset hut for a decade and have no idea what they are seeing here.

God FaceTimes the boy at seven in the morning. She wants to know how the interviews are going.

Over the years, Dick has acquired more and more charging cables and power bricks. He has them plugged in all over the house. He can go into any room and, with very little fuss, plug in his phone and charge it for a while. He likes to plug it in in the living room while he sits on the couch googling women he used to know. Then he checks for messages and takes the phone to the kitchen, where he plugs it into the USB outlet he's installed next to the refrigerator.

The boy is sitting on the living room couch with the cat. The cat is asleep with its chin on its front paws, its back legs twitching occasionally. The girl is out somewhere buying something. The boy tries to gather her together in his mind. What he comes up with seems like the hollowest of constructions, a thing he might fallaciously rely upon to support him, only to find himself hanging in thin air, about to fall to his death in a chaos of misunderstanding. He puts his hand on the cat and lets his image of the girl blow away like the last bit of smoke from a fire that has been burning all night in spite of a mighty wind but has given up now, gasping its last grey breath. 'It's like I can touch something in my head that matters,' the boy tells the cat, 'but it never touches me back.'

The girl sets her book down on the couch. She looks at the cat sleeping in her lap. Then she looks up at the boy. 'Come,' she says. 'Sit here beside me and help me pet the cat.'

The boy puts his hand on the girl. The girl waits. The boy lifts his face. The girl puts her hand on the boy's arm. 'When you're scared,' says the boy, 'do you feel like you can't move?' The girl says nothing. 'It's like everything fills me up so full,' says the boy, 'that it's equal to me. Like I'm nothing more than everything that fills me up. I can't step outside myself and touch the things that confront me. I can't touch myself.' The boy looks around the room. 'Everything becomes nothing,' he says. 'The air smells of fear. The bed is a memory. The rain splattering on the window ledge in the bedroom takes me back to when I was a kid. It's like my toothbrush in the cup in the bathroom has always been there, since the dawn of time. Like the sound of the fan in our bedroom is something cosmic. And the cone of light from my bedside lamp, it's the sun. The things that come out of my body, the things that come out of my mouth, the laughs and groans and all the crap I say, it all means nothing. The words that pour out of me endlessly. The pain I sometimes feel in my left knee when I get out of bed in the morning. The little sprouts of black hair on the backs of my knuckles that seem to be getting thicker.'

'What did you do while you were gone?' asks the interviewer. The boy looks away. 'Well, I wasn't giving up,' he says. 'But I did stay very still for a time and mourn. I felt a deep, irreversible sadness that I tried not to run away from. It was hard to sit still at first. I tried not to anticipate my next move, or think about how I could escape. I did think about going downstairs to the kitchen to get something to eat, but then I remembered I wasn't in the house. I told myself, "Just sit still for a moment. You don't need a snack." I wanted to wait a while, then get up suddenly, with no clear idea of what I was about to do, or where I was going to go. I wanted to blunder into the world, the way a drunk blunders into other people's lives, wreaking havoc.'

God is back in their garage and she's brought along the new god. 'Did you invite her back?' the girl asks. 'No,' says the boy. He gives her a pleading look. 'They just showed up,' he says. 'I swear it.' 'I can hear them talking down there when I'm in the kitchen,' says the girl. 'You need to get rid of them for good.' The boy goes down and finds the new god interviewing the old God at the back of the garage. 'Why do you spell your name with a capital G?' the new god is asking. The new god seems very young in this light. Her tone of voice is almost belligerent. The old God smiles benignly but says nothing. 'It seems a bit presumptuous, don't you think?' asks the new god. The old God shrugs. 'It's just a thing I've always done,' she says mildly. 'I've done it since the dawn of time.' She laughs. 'Old habits,' she says. 'You know how it is.' She pauses, then adds: 'I think you're reading too much into this.' The new god doesn't say anything, just scowls. She turns to the boy. 'What are you guys cooking up there?' she asks. 'It smells so good.' She turns to the old God. 'We should go up there and say hi to the girl.' The old God nods. 'Good idea,' she says. The new god shuts off her camera, which is just her phone, and unplugs the spotlight she has trained on the old God. The boy recognizes the spotlight. It's his work light, which he had forgotten was out here, so he's glad to see it's getting some use. The girl looks displeased when she sees the three of them arrive in the kitchen. 'Hi,' the new god says brightly. 'Hello,' says the girl coldly. 'It smells so good in here,' says the new god. 'It sure does,' says the old God. The boy says nothing. The girl drops her shoulders. 'I'm making cinnamon buns,' she says. 'You want some coffee with them?'

Dick looks out the window. There are fluffy white clouds painted all across the sky. There is a woman sleeping in the bed behind him. Dick can hear air coming out of her nose. The plan had been to take a nap. They would both go to sleep, and when they awoke they would feel better. But Dick hasn't been able to sleep. And now he is feeling lonely. *Is it my fault the clouds look the way they look today?* he thinks with a sudden jab of anger.

The boy reads aloud from the newspaper. The girl sits on the edge of the bed in a towel. Clouds drift by outside.

The boy is working on a new list of rules. It's 6:00 a.m. He hears the girl. She's moving around upstairs. He looks up from his cereal and listens, trying to figure out what she will do next. It's early for her to be up. He hears the bedroom door open, then the thump of the cat landing on the floor of the hall. The door closes and the house is silent. The cat arrives and sits by the boy's feet looking miffed. The boy picks up his pen and begins formulating a rule about early mornings and the cat.

'Do you mind if I sit here?' the boy asks. The girl looks up at him like he's crazy. She seems nervous. She lifts her knapsack off the seat and onto her lap, then sits motionless, staring at the back of the seat in front of her. The boy sits. He wants to try to see her face again. There is something about her face today. He leans forward a little. But she's got her head bowed over at an angle so that all the boy can see is the cone of her hood jutting out past her face.

'He's not really called the captain, although this is what I've decided to call him,' the boy tells the girl. They are standing outside the front door, about to go down to the car. The sky is a washed-out blue. The boy scratches his nose. Then he says, 'There really isn't any good reason to call him the captain.' The girl locks the front door. She shifts her purse on her shoulder. The two of them descend the concrete steps to the driveway. When they are standing on either side of the car, the girl looks across at the boy. 'It's Dick again, isn't it?' she says. 'This guy you call the captain. He's actually Dick, right?' The cat is inside the house, sitting at the window watching them.

The boy is almost asleep. He's not sure what the girl is saying is actual words. It might be more like an incantation. He tries to wake himself properly, but he seems to be stuck in some half-world with no immediate chance of revival.

The girl holds the boy's face. She feels a subterranean trembling that originates deep inside him. It comes up through his cheeks and enters the girl through her hands. A sympathetic quivering arises inside her. She pulls the boy's face close. She puts her lips against his cheek. 'Where the fuck have you been?' she whispers harshly, not really expecting an answer, but getting one in the savagery of his response.

'Every word arrives partly out of what precedes it, and partly out of thin air,' says the girl, 'and it's the part that comes out of thin air that you can't ever seem to capture.' Then she is silent, looking into the air in front of her, as though waiting for another word to come along and help her out. The boy leans over and opens the drawer of his bedside table. He gets out a pen and paper. 'That would make a good rule,' he says, before writing down what the girl just said.

The boy hears a voice. It's coming from the TV. The TV is downstairs. The boy imagines the face out of which the voice is issuing. It's the face of God. For a long time there is nothing. Then the girl says something into the silence that lies between them like a messenger arrived to pass along the nothing they are silently slipping toward together like skaters falling off the edge of a lake.

The message is etched into a flat rock: *When you see a river, turn into the woods and continue on to the biggest boulder. I've left you a package there. They are closing in now. It won't be long. If you take the northern pass, you should be able to evade them.* There is a stain on the rock that looks like blood, as though the person who left the message has written it by severing a part of their own body, pulling out the bone to use as a chisel. Dick is pretty sure that's a finger bone sitting by the rock. But it might also be a finger-shaped rock. The person who wrote the message is long since dead, Dick knows. The intended recipient: also dead. 'It's a message,' says Dick, still astride his horse. 'What's it say?' asks Dick's mother. She's wearing a cowboy hat with a string she can cinch up around her chin. 'I don't think it matters what the message says,' says Dick. 'I do,' says Dick's mother. 'I can't really read it very well,' Dick says, even though he is pretty sure he has just read it perfectly. The day grows dark. Black clouds race across the sky. Later, when they've set up camp for the night, Dick's mother comes into the tent with a tin plate of homemade oatmeal raisin cookies and a canteen full of milk.

The phone rings. It's the boy. 'They are coming,' he tells the girl, 'late Saturday night. Or, rather, early Sunday. And they will stay in a hotel overnight. I will call you when I get back.' 'Okay,' says the girl, although she has no idea who 'they' are, or where the boy is calling from, or why he isn't at home in their bedroom where he usually is at this time of night.

It's the middle of winter. The boy is lying naked on the bed with the window wide open. 'Do you even own any pants?' asks the girl. 'And I don't mean PJ bottoms.' The boy scratches his leg. 'We're going for a walk,' says the girl. 'I have to go to the mall. I need buttons.' She goes out of the room. Eventually the boy gets up and roots around on the bedroom floor, trying to find some pants, but then he hears the front door slam shut and he knows he's too late.

Dick steps out of the car and stands for a while in a place beyond time. He leans on the open car door and looks up the dusty gravel road, trying to will someone or something to appear out of the sunshine that is streaming across the cornfields. He finds himself wanting to see his mother again, although he doesn't even have any really good idea what she might look like now. He's been away from her for so long. *She was beautiful in the way those birch leaves over there are beautiful from a distance,* he tells himself, trying to conjure her in words. In his mind, his mother looks like an angel descending in a cone of light. Like she's brought her own cone of light to the party. She has very dark hair now, and the gown he imagines her wearing is white. And she has on those little white shoes with the strange heels that she used to wear all the time.

'Lift your head,' says the boy. The girl lifts her head. 'A little more to the left,' says the boy, dipping his head to see in under the girl's eyebrows. The girl moves her head a little to the left. The boy moves his face closer to the girl's. 'Now hold still,' he says. The girl doesn't move. 'How was your walk this morning?' she asks the boy nervously, just trying to make a little conversation. 'Don't move,' says the boy. The girl goes silent. The boy pulls back. 'There's a secret rule in there,' he says, looking straight into the girl's eyes. 'It's stuck at the back of your left eye. We need to get it out of there and write it down.'

The boy is lying on his back in bed. The room is dark. He has his hand on the cat. The cat is lying under the sheet with its back against his leg. The boy whispers something soothing to the cat. He can feel the cat purring. *Maybe something in me has changed*, he thinks. He tries to remember if he felt anything change in the night. Has he felt anything change? But if something has changed, maybe it changed while he was sleeping. In which case maybe he wouldn't have felt it change. Or maybe he felt it in his sleep but didn't remember it when he woke up in the morning, like a dream that slips away just as you are sure you are about to remember it.

The cat sits on the patio, staring at the screen door. Then it goes over to the grass and flops over on its side. It looks back at the boy overtop of its fur. The boy takes a drink of water from a glass he has sitting on the table next to the lounge chair he is in. 'What is your soul, anyway?' he says to the cat after he's set his water back down on the table. 'Isn't it just the sounds you hear inside your head that can't be given any words?' He watches the cat roll onto its back. 'Your soul is the sound that can't be given any words, ever.' The cat is upside down now, staring at the boy with its ears crushed into the grass. 'And what is God but the way the world can move around inside you, like a kitten under a blanket. The way the world can move around inside you without your consent.' The little fountain is running in the corner of the yard, making tiny gurgling noises. The cat gets up and goes over to lick some water. The boy watches it for a while, then closes his eyes and dreams of a time in his life that hasn't happened yet and probably never will.

'Why don't you use one of those to mic yourself?' asks the girl, pointing at a row of microphones in the interviewer's equipment case. The interviewer is back for a fourth interview. 'I can never understand what you're saying when you ask a question,' says the girl. The interviewer straightens up and faces the girl. 'I do that on purpose,' she says. 'Why?' asks the girl. 'My husband thinks it's better that way,' says the interviewer. 'And so do I,' she adds. 'But I can never understand what you're saying,' says the girl. 'Exactly,' says the interviewer. She looks down, then back up at the girl. Scratches at her chin. 'It's more startling this way,' she says. 'We don't like anything that explains itself too well,' she adds. 'We don't trust explanations.' She turns to the boy. 'Ready?' she asks.

Dick has to go off the sidewalk and onto people's lawns to keep from getting a soaker. Every time there is less water on the sidewalk and he gets back beside his mother, she sticks out her tongue and laps it across the palm of her hand, then reaches over to try to make some of the pieces of Dick's hair that are sticking up on his head go down and stay.

The boy is standing on a chair in the bedroom. 'It looks like something died inside this light bulb,' he says. The girl looks up. 'Gross,' she says. 'Are those spider legs?' she asks. 'I hope not,' says the boy. He keeps moving his head around, trying to get a better look inside the light bulb. 'Yuck,' says the girl, ducking her head and hurrying across the room. The boy unscrews the light bulb and holds it close. 'It's probably just a couple filaments come loose,' he says, looking back, only to discover the girl standing behind the bedroom door looking scared.

'Listen,' says the boy to the girl, putting his finger to his lips when she comes around the car to stand beside him in the parking lot at the mall. 'Just listen.' The boy feels like what they are hearing now is a sound that comes from beyond the place where you can actually hear any sounds. The girl listens. She hears flags flapping in the wind at the entrance to the mall. She hears a couple of kids whining, a mother telling them to stop. She hears the boy breathe out beside her. Then she hears her own feet on the pavement as she steps away from the boy toward the mall, not all that sure she wants him to follow.

After the woman Dick just bought a drink for has gotten up and crossed the bar, and Dick can no longer hear the clicking of her heels on the hardwood floor, he drains off the last of his whisky and sits where he is for a while, feeling like he's missed some opportunity. *I should have asked her a question,* he thinks. *I should have asked her … what? What could I have asked her? How long did it take you to get your hair to go like that? Do you trim your own eyebrows? What colour lipstick is that?*

The boy moves around and around the coffee table, keeping his eyes on the girl. The girl is getting dizzy from watching him. Finally, the boy stops and sits down on the couch across from her. He picks up a cushion that's sitting on the couch beside him and squishes it into his lap. The girl's eyes look clear and wet, like they are about to spill out of her face. There's no right way to do this, they both know. They feel like they can't touch each other right now. They need to make up a new way of doing things. 'I have wandered out the back door of my life,' whispers the boy, 'only to find that memory is the enemy.'

Dick is having an adventure when the woman he's been sleeping with wakes him up. 'You were dreaming,' says the woman. The woman in Dick's dream was naked. Dick can't remember what lent everything that glow he saw in his dream, or how these brilliant-edged disks have gotten under his eyelids, or how to get them out now that he is awake again. 'Was I in the dream?' asks the woman. 'Was I naked?

'There was no late at night, really,' says the boy, 'but it always felt a little like night.' The interviewer waits. 'It didn't really feel like anything,' the boy adds. He looks at the interviewer. She's wearing a yellow dress that makes her look like a flower he could pick and put in a vase for the girl. She's very tiny. 'I tried to remember myself,' says the boy, 'as someone who could lie awake at night. I tried to think of myself – ' He stops, as though his train of thought has trailed away into the woods way up north somewhere where the train doesn't go. 'Well, I couldn't really think of myself at all,' he says, finally. The interviewer waits. But the boy stays quiet. And then he stands. The interviewer reaches for the camera, turns it off. The boy starts to say something. The interviewer holds up her hand. 'Wait,' she says, 'not without the camera.' She reaches. 'I was just going to ask if you want some coffee,' says the boy. The interviewer regards the boy, then seems to come to some sort of decision. 'Sure, I'd love some coffee,' she says. She trains the camera on the boy as he goes to work making the coffee. 'Where's your wife today?' she asks. The boy shrugs. 'I don't know,' he says. 'She doesn't confess her plans to me like she used to.'

The boy comes home with a new rule. He has it written down on a piece of paper. He hands it to the girl when they meet up in the kitchen just before dinner. The girl unfolds the little scrap of paper and reads what it says. She looks at the boy. 'No,' she says, very quietly. She looks down at the piece of paper. 'I'm not doing this,' she says. She extends the hand that's holding the paper toward the boy, tentatively, as though she is proffering a morsel of food to a starving panther, hoping it will take it and go away without eating her. The boy takes the paper and looks down at what he's written. For a long time, he doesn't move. Then he folds the paper carefully and puts it back in his pocket.

'It's like someone points a gun at you,' says the boy, 'and they say, "Come with me," and you go, not because you are afraid they will shoot you – because you know they won't, they can't, they don't have a gun, there is no gun, the gun is a phantasm, it doesn't exist, they don't exist, not because they are made up, even if they are made up – but because they raise in you the spectre of a person with a gun and you acquiesce, not to the person holding the gun, because there is no person holding a gun, but to the thing in you that wants to be pointed at.'

The boy likes to pretend that the girl's boobs are their sons, Nim and Nom. 'Are the kids staying up all night?' the boy asks. The girl is sitting up in bed with her top off. 'I don't know,' she says. 'They don't confess their plans to me like they used to.' The boy laughs a little, nervously, like he and the girl are on their way to a costume party and they are going as a couple of nudists. 'You look cold,' the boy says. He's standing beside the bed. 'I am cold,' says the girl. She looks at the boy. 'Aren't you?' she asks. 'Yes,' says the boy. 'We should put our clothes back on,' says the girl. The boy nods, then gets down onto the bed next to the girl and lays his head on her stomach. He can hear the gurgling of secret messages her body is delivering to him.

Across the sandy expanse in front of where Dick and his mother sit on a towel, the universe dissolves into spray above waves that tumble onto the beach like steamrollers emerging through early-morning fog out of the bowels of the earth to crush things flat enough to make it easier for everyone to get around without a lot of inconvenience.

The boy puts on a hat. 'Wrong hat,' he mumbles. He stands up from the bench in the hall. 'I need a different hat,' he says. He looks around. He throws the hat down and sits. He stands. Puts on another hat. He stuffs his hands into his pockets, grabs them from the inside and pulls, turning them inside out. Stuff falls to the floor. The boy looks down. Dick's pockets hang at his sides like colostomy bags. The new hat is too big and goes down over his eyes. He can't see anything. He turns his head sideways so that his chin juts over his shoulder. The furnace comes on. The smell of heat rises from the vent in the floor. The boy puts his fingers to his cheeks, as though he is a blind man learning his own face. Some hair that he isn't expecting touches his fingers where it has escaped from under Dick's hat.

'I keep trying to remember everything I said today,' the boy tells the girl. 'Trying to write it all down.' He is sitting at his desk with his journal open in front of him and a pen in his hand. He looks up. The girl is standing in the doorway, holding a glass of milk. There are bits of chocolate on her face.

The boy is in the bedroom, wearing only his red flannel PJ bottoms. He is interviewing the girl, who is wearing her bathrobe. 'You have to keep going,' says the girl, 'no matter how you feel, no matter how bad things look, you have to keep going. You have to do the job you remember yourself doing the last time you felt you were doing a job worth doing.'

'Is that your answer to question two, or are you still answering question one?' the boy asks. A long time later, he looks up from his notes and sees that the girl is gone. He listens to the silence she's left behind and wonders if it is relief he is feeling, or a sort of bereavement. *Maybe relief and bereavement are closer together than I'd like to believe*, he thinks before going off to the bathroom to fill the tub.

The girl comes down the stairs slowly, still waking up. Halfway down, she stops to stretch. She looks down, sees the boy standing at the bottom of the stairs. She freezes, her arms still in the air from her stretch. 'You look different,' says the boy. The girl lowers her arms gradually, as though the boy is a cop who might shoot her if she makes any sudden moves. Outside, on the road, some-one coughs.

Dick's face dips forward into the blue light of his phone. The plumber he hired to fix his kitchen sink bangs on something. She reaches out and grabs a small wrench from the floor, then ducks back into the cupboard. Her bum sticks up, facing Dick. She makes a noise of disgust at something under the sink. 'I don't even care anymore,' she says. She pulls her head out and sits on the floor facing Dick, her legs sticking out like two sides of a triangle. Strands of hair have pulled free from her scrunchie and she pushes at them with the sides of her arms.

The girl is asleep in bed. She's almost sixty. But to the boy she still looks like a little girl. She looks wiry and stubborn, a mule of a dirty-faced kid bent on riding her bike straight through the middle of the forbidden forest. But then, the girl isn't there at all, is she? Even when she is right there in front of him, he can't seem to arrange things in his head to make her become more real, more of what she really is. He can't empty things out of his head enough to really find her.

The girl watches the way the boy moves his fingers. She doesn't see it when he lifts his greying eyebrows and opens his eyes wide, like he has just discovered the reason for things falling, and it isn't gravity.

Singing a little song, the boy holds his hands over his ears. The voices he's trying to block out are made up of words trying to get out of his head, like sentences going the wrong way out through his ear canals. The boy is bleeding words out through the channels of his ears back into the world, like debris floating on a river, meandering out to the sea.

The woman Dick is dating looks nice in her new hat with her hair pinned up under it and her dangly earrings. Dick stands before her like a puppet gone limp after the puppeteer has suffered a fatal heart attack.

The girl is not a dream. She exists. But, at the same time, she isn't there. The boy knows she isn't there. The girl is an opalescent membrane that the boy can fill or not. *It doesn't matter*, the boy dreams. 'I walked down to the river and sat,' he says. 'My bum felt damp.' The girl is the river. The boy can feel her swirl around him, her hands darting like fish. His desire becomes the river. He wants to drink the girl, feel her sliding down his throat. Have her swimming through his bloodstream.

'It's like we're exploring,' says the boy hoarsely. *The girl will hear the tone of my voice*, the boy thinks. *She won't hear the words.* 'We are exploring the river,' says the boy. The girl shakes the boy's arm gently and the boy sits up.

'What did you do yesterday while I was out?' asks the girl. 'Sat on the couch,' says the boy. 'That's it?' asks the girl. 'Mostly,' says the boy.

The boy shrugs, then grins. He leans in close to the girl and talks. He goes on for a long time, gesturing and gesticulating. The girl leans away from him in the bed and looks toward the window like a prisoner waiting for the paddy wagon to slow down so she can jump out the back. The boy gets out a piece of paper from his bedside table and draws some diagrams. He is trying hard to explain. 'What do you mean?' asks the girl, breathing out loudly through her nose. 'What are you drawing?' She sounds alarmed. 'Are these more of your rules?' The boy looks down at her, at the book she has lying open on her stomach. He looks back at his drawings, traces the lines with his forefinger. He has no idea what he is trying to draw. He doesn't know anything. This, in fact, is what he's trying to tell the girl, what he's been trying to tell her all along.

Morning arrives. The boy sits up. He's in bed, hair askew, eyes bleary. The girl is beside him, still slumbering, the bedcovers crumpled around her feet, like she's dead and needs the boy to pull the sheets up over her head.

The boy asks a question. When the girl answers, it feels to her as though she is having a conversation with herself, a conversation that the boy is merely translating. It's as though the boy has known the answers to his questions all his life and wants simply to confirm what he already knows.

The girl holds up her hand, as if to ask a question. 'Yes,' says the boy, 'you, at the back.' The girl giggles. The boy wakes up. He gets out of bed and walks around the room. The girl is somewhere nearby. He can hear her talking to the cat, but she doesn't see him. She thinks he has disappeared. And he has. And then the boy doesn't see the girl, even as he finds her again where she has always been. He will always be without the girl, even when he is right there within her.

The boy holds the girl by her hair. He feels her fear. *She would taste like bread*, he thinks.

'I'm a different person than the person you think I am,' says the voice on the phone. 'So you're saying I have the wrong number,' says the girl. 'No,' says the voice, 'I'm just saying I'm different from who you think I am.' The girl is pretty sure she's dialled home and that it's the voice of the boy she's hearing on the phone. 'Okay,' she says, when the boy says nothing more. 'Maybe I'll try to call you later.' 'Okay,' says the boy.

The girl looks for a moment like she is going to say something. She pauses from eating her cereal, spoon aloft near her mouth. A drop of milk falls, splattering gently into the cereal bowl.

'It's real foggy out there,' says the boy. The girl joins him at the window. She can't see anything beyond the ghostly outline of the trees that are just beyond their balcony. They stand together like that for a long time.

The boy nods toward the place where the sun is going down. The girl sees the message written across the sun, but she can't keep looking at it long enough to figure out what it says. 'What does it say?' she asks. The boy looks at the message for a second, then back at the girl. 'I don't know,' he says. 'I don't think I can read it without going blind.'

'In your eyes, your front yard recombines, and there is a pop in the back of your mind,' says Dick. The woman sitting across from Dick at a little table in a café downtown looks up sleepily, like she's fallen out of time, only to find herself trapped in a world she doesn't recognize with this Dick guy.

'There's something coming toward us like wind,' says the boy. He gets up off the bed and leaves the room. The house is quiet. The silence feels thick, like heavy water. The boy pictures himself struggling to move through the silence, as though he is up to his neck in it, about to drown.

The boy looks out the window. A pickup truck drives by slowly, scattering salt. A man with a shovel is digging a hole at the end of the street.

'You weren't expecting me, were you?' asks the boy. The girl looks confused. They've arranged to meet here. 'I don't mean that as a description of my entrance,' the boy explains, laughing. 'I mean it as an announcement of my arrival.' He is wearing a hat the girl has never seen, something like a beret. 'I don't mean this as an announcement of my arrival here today,' the boy elaborates. 'I mean it as an announcement of my arrival here on earth.' He smiles broadly. 'But I knew you were coming,' says the girl. 'You told me to meet you here.'

The boy is forcing the blood back into the life of the planet, losing his own life for the sake of his friend, the world. The world is the boy's new friend that accompanies the boy everywhere he goes.

The girl is at the kitchen table. She watches the boy through hooded eyes. The boy says something. The girl yawns. The boy drops a scoop of ice cream off a wooden spoon. It falls into a ceramic bowl. The girl looks down at her hands, then back up at the boy. Outside, a leaf falls from a tree in the front yard.

The boy is trapped. Falling. Dropping away. The girl is a blank oval. She is dark nothingness. But then, inside the darkness, the boy sees a little light. He follows it.

The girl pulls a hairbrush slowly through her hair. 'Where is the forbidden forest?' she asks. The boy is staring down at the journal he has open in his lap. 'In Denver,' he says without looking up.

The girl wakes to find the boy standing at the bedroom window. 'The sun is coming,' he says. The girl sits up and wipes the sleep out of her eyes, then drops back onto the bed like it might be able to stop her from falling.

It's hardly a service to the boy to keep him alive if he exists only as a series of moments stored in the girl's head. *Sure, he exists,* thinks the girl. The girl knows the boy exists. As long as she holds on to him in her mind, the boy will continue to exist. But unless she can feel him pressed up against her, unless they can cross this divide, unless they can bridge this rift that's keeping them apart even now that the boy has come back, the boy can only ever really exist for the girl as a sort of sickness.

The girl remembers a morning around the time of their eighth anniversary when she made a quiet plan to leave the boy.

'I remembered something this morning,' the boy tells the girl, 'so I went upstairs, but by the time I got there, it didn't matter anymore.' The girl sticks her fork into her chicken, then just leaves it there, standing up like a stop sign.

When he is finished doing his business, the boy gets up and looks in the toilet. It's full of words. He thinks about reaching in and getting a few out, maybe trying to do something with them, create something, but he is afraid the girl might catch him, so he closes the toilet, stands in silence beside it for a moment, then flushes, muttering a quiet apology under his breath.

Across town, someone is cutting grass, the mower howling loud and distant like a creature caught roaring in a jar. The boy and the girl are standing on the balcony, side by side at the railing, watching the sun go down behind the ravine. 'I don't know what to say to you anymore,' says the girl. The boy stares out into the distance beyond the ravine. 'I've never run out of things to say to you,' he says. In the distance the tops of trees undulate gently in the wind.

When the boy leaves to go to the dry cleaner, the girl stays in the kitchen, waiting. Outside, the sun is setting and the street lights are coming on. Cars drive by. The mall will be closing soon.

Words fall from the sky like snow. They make patterns on the grass. The boy and the girl watch to find out what the words will tell them. But the patterns aren't grammatical. Or geometrical. Or graphical. The boy stays silent, gazing out the living room window, the girl beside him, looking from the falling words to the light reflected in the boy's eyes. In the distance of the boy's eyes, she sees a single sentence drift like dandelion detritus in a windy field. She points. The boy looks. The sentence writhes out of rhythm, then disappears into random word clouds patterned across the sky.

At the last moment, thinks the boy, *right before the moment when there are no more moments, I'm sure I will finally come awake.*

'The first time I saw you,' the boy tells the girl, 'I saw you from the back. You were walking across the dance floor at that club we used to go to north of town. I wanted to take your clothes off.' The girl turns her head. They are side by side in bed. The old cat is lying on the boy's feet, soaking up his warmth. 'I wanted to take your shirt off.' The boy hesitates. 'I wanted to see the angular place where your shoulder blade sticks out from your back when you lift your arm,' he says.

The boy remembers lingering in the girl's driveway a few days after he met her, not wanting to go home, feeling like he and the girl were just young opportunities dressed up in flesh, standing in the cool dark of night.

'I wanted to go on adventures when we were younger,' says the boy. 'But I was always pretty afraid.' 'Really?' asks the girl. 'I always thought I was the one who was afraid. Like when we were in the airport in Athens and there were all those army guys with guns everywhere.' 'That scared me, too,' says the boy. 'I never knew that,' says the girl. 'I know,' says the boy. 'I knew you were scared and I was afraid if I admitted that I was scared too, you'd turn around and get back on a plane to go home.' 'I'm glad we stayed,' says the girl. 'Me too,' says the boy. 'We had fun.' 'Remember the motorcycle?' asks the girl. The boy laughs. 'It was more of a minibike,' he says. 'Or a moped.' 'Still,' says the girl. 'Yeah,' says the boy.

They don't think it could possibly matter. But they discuss it anyway. They hear wind. The sun will come up soon. The boy knows what the girl used to look like. He can still picture her the way she was. Her face. Her hair. Her body. The way she stretched out beneath him. The way her neck emerged from her clothing. And her hands. He remembers she took her mitts off in the car. Then she put them back on again and they got out of the car together. It was a blue car.

'I want you to be honest with me,' the girl tells the boy. 'I really do,' she adds. She takes a bite of her toast, lifts her shoulders in a shrug. 'Of course I want you to be honest with me,' she says. She seems almost tearful, but if she is going to cry, it won't be for him, the boy knows. She picks up her mug and takes a sip of coffee. She swallows. 'So now you've been honest with me,' she says. 'Now I know you're disgusting.' She looks at the boy. 'Are you happy?' Dick looks down at the floor. 'No,' he says. He sits down at the table across from the little girl he hasn't seen since he was ten and watches the way the toast goes into her mouth.

A train stops behind the house where the boy and the girl are living. The boy sits up. The lamp on the bedside table trembles. It's spring and the window is open. The noise from the train is deafening. The boy smells diesel exhaust. It feels like the world is ending. Or just beginning. He looks down at the girl who is asleep on the bed beside him and realizes he's alone.

EPILOGUE

A couple of months after they got married, the girl and the boy were riding home on the subway when the angel sat down between them. It was like God had answered some kind of prayer they'd been making. The angel was achingly tiny with a big homemade pompom on the top of her hat. She pushed her way between the boy and the girl, and then promptly fell asleep. Each time the subway stopped at a station, the angel swayed against the boy; and then when they pulled away from the station again, she swayed against the girl. They felt so happy to be riding through the city in the subway, crowded into this seat with the angel, that they stayed on the train long past their stop, just to be there. The angel woke once, about two stops before the end of the line. She pulled out a Kleenex from her bag and held it to her nose for a moment. Then she shoved it into a pocket, dropped her head forward, and fell back to sleep.

Ken Sparling is the author of six novels: *Dad Says He Saw You at the Mall*, commissioned by Gordon Lish; *Hush Up and Listen Stinky Poo Butt*, handmade using discarded library books and a sewing machine; a novel with no title; *For Those Whom God Has Blessed with Fingers*; *Book*, which was shortlisted for the Trillium Award; *Intention | Implication | Wind*; and *This Poem Is a House*. He lives in Richmond Hill, Ontario, and shares his handmade books at kensparling.ca and on Instagram @kensparling.

Typeset in Albertina and Graphie.

Printed at the Coach House on bpNichol Lane in Toronto, Ontario, on Zephyr
Antique Laid paper, which was manufactured, acid-free, in Saint-Jérôme, Quebec,
from second-growth forests. This book was printed with vegetable-based ink
on a 1973 Heidelberg KORD offset litho press. Its pages were folded on a Baum-
folder, gathered by hand, bound on a Sulby Auto-Minabinda, and trimmed on a
Polar single-knife cutter.

Coach House is on the traditional territory of many nations, including the Mississaugas of the Credit, the Anishnabeg, the Chippewa, the Haudenosaunee, and
the Wendat peoples, and is now home to many diverse First Nations, Inuit, and
Métis peoples. We acknowledge that Toronto is covered by Treaty 13 with the
Mississaugas of the Credit. We are grateful to live and work on this land.

Edited by Pasha Malla and Alana Wilcox
Cover design by Crystal Sikma
Interior design by Crystal Sikma
Author photo by Stephen Sparling

Coach House Books
80 bpNichol Lane
Toronto ON M5S 3J4
Canada

416 979 2217
800 367 6360

mail@chbooks.com
www.chbooks.com